The Protege

Kailin Gow

The Protégé by Kailin Gow

The Protege
Published by Kailin Gow
Copyright © 2013 Kailin Gow

For information, please contact:
Kailingowbooks(at)aol(dot)com.
First Edition.
Printed in the United States of America.

ISBN: 978-1-59748-077-2

DEDICATION

This dedication to my husband whose love makes all things possible.

This book series is also dedicated to all the women and children of domestic abuse and violence. Hope this series will bring some comfort and hope to you or someone you know in some way.

Prologue

The small but elegantly furnished luxury apartment was neat and tidy except for Serena's bedroom. Three skirts lay on her bed; the red one too frilly, the black one too short, and white one too summery. Atop them lay a variety of shirts and blouses including a few that were simply too revealing, one that was too festive and another that looked too frumpy on her.

In front of the open closet were shoes and sandals of every color. One after the other Serena had discarded them. Her dressing table was strewn with brushes, combs, hairpins and bottles of hairspray and mousse. For all the time she'd spent in front of the mirror debating how to set her hair, she'd finally pulled her long thick dark hair back into a prim and proper chignon. As for make-up, she'd decided that minimalism was the way to go; a swipe of mascara and a touch of pale lipstick. Nothing gaudy, nothing showy, nothing to show the professor but her intelligent brown eyes and eager expression.

"Hopefully that'll impress him," she'd muttered as she'd left the mirror to dress.

Today was too important to screw up. More than anything Serena wanted to look right and impress her potential adviser. Although recently transferred, this was her senior year in her undergraduate studies, and she needed a graduate adviser. She already had the necessary credits to start graduate level courses. If her meeting went well, she'd transition into her graduate studies early, keep the same adviser and finish her studies a year in advance.

Peering into her closet she made a last ditch attempt to find something suitable. Her hand came to rest on a calf length navy blue pencil skirt.

Very professional, she thought. *Very academic. Very studious and serious. Yes. This will do.*

She pulled the snug, but not too tight skirt on and pulled the zipper up. The effect was exactly what she was looking for. All that remained was finding the perfect button down shirt to go with it; and she knew exactly which one she needed. She pushed all the hangers to one end of the closet and found a perfectly crisp and immaculately white shirt.

"Who could possibly turn me down now?" she asked of her reflection once she'd buttoned the shirt up and tucked it into her skirt. She looked every bit like an ideal graduate student…academic, smart, and serious about her studies.

Pleased with herself, she hopped into her slightly tight, conservative two-inch black pumps, grabbed her handbag and headed out to the apartment building's parking lot. Her small black Mini Cooper was parked clear across the lot, but Serena enjoyed the few moments of brisk, cool autumn air, despite the tight squeeze of her toes.

Her stride restricted by the narrow skirt, she took small, dainty steps to the car, but when she opened the car door, she paused before getting in. How was she going to maneuver into the low car when she had so little freedom of movement? Remembering pictures she'd once seen of Princess Diana when she was very little at her grandmother's, getting elegantly into a car, she turned her back to the driver seat and sat down, then swiveled around to face the steering wheel.

"Here's to trying to be a true lady," she said with pride as she tossed her handbag onto the passenger seat.

Feeling excited and anxious, she drove the familiar route to the campus. For three years she'd lived in this apartment. For three years, she driven down Harbor Boulevard, turned onto the San Diego Freeway and maneuvered her car through traffic until Jamboree Road; though when traffic was too heavy, she'd take MacArthur Boulevard instead.

Today Jamboree Road would do. Traffic was only marginally heavy, but mostly fluid and she arrived at the campus with more than enough time to spare. Smiling and pleased with herself, she pulled into the parking lot only to find that it was jam packed with cars. Though she circled and circled, every parking space was filled. Finally, at the far end of the lot, she spotted a woman walking to her car. Serena hurried to follow her, hoping the woman would vacate a space.

As Serena pulled up beside her, the woman looked at her with a displeased expression.

"Excuse me," Serena called out as she hurried to roll down her window. "Are you leaving the lot? There isn't a vacant space in the whole place."

7

Pursing her lips, the woman nodded, but seemed in no hurry to get to her car.

Serena bit her lip and resisted the urge to beg the woman to walk a little faster.

After a torturous minute, the woman arrived at her car, started the engine and slowly pulled out. Having lost enough time, Serena pulled into the space and hurried out of the car only to hear a slight tearing sound in the process. She gritted her teeth. Of all the days…

She looked down at her skirt for any sign of damage, reassured herself that everything looked fine and walked as quickly as the narrow skirt would allow. With the administrators building looming in the distance, she suddenly regretted her wardrobe choice. An A-line skirt would have allowed easier movement.

The clip clop of her heels indicated she was walking fast enough, but still the building remained discouragingly far. Hoping no one would notice her, she jacked up her skirt to her thighs and took long strides that quickly had her at the door.

Her feet ached and her back was moist with sweat, but she'd made it. Taking a quick second to cool her brow, she gazed at her reflection in the window. Her neatly tucked in blouse now looked like she'd slept in it and wild tendrils of hair had escaped her meticulously pinned chignon. "Damn it," she groaned as she licked her fingers and tried to tame the locks back toward the chignon.

Muttering her displeasure at the parking lot situation, she hurried to the adviser's door on the second floor.

She knocked firmly on the door; too firmly, she realized. He'll think she was being belligerent.

"Come in." His voice was at once commanding and authoritative, while having a strangely husky and sexy undertone. It ran over her entire body like a soft and sensual touch, making her want to stand at attention and let whoever owned that voice to do whatever he wanted with her.

The image of a young professor, with thick and short cropped, dark locks, piercing grey eyes and a body built for seduction immediately came to her mind, but she quickly shook it off as she opened the door.

However, the stunningly attractive man behind the oversized mahogany desk did not disappoint. As she'd imagined, his hair was dark, almost black, but it fell to his shoulders. His eyes were blue, bright and intelligent, fringed with dark lashes that heightened the intensity in his eyes, disarmingly direct and beautiful as though he could see deep into her. His lips were naturally full and pouty, sensual and sexy, the kind of lips you want to kiss and suck on all day. Confident, almost arrogant, he seemed completely at home in the office that was rich with cherry oak bookshelves and an expensive looking oriental rug.

The tiffany lamp on his desk offered a warm amber glow that offset his cool blue glare, slightly angry and annoyed.

"You must be Miss Serena Singleton." Her name was said with an unfamiliar but sexy accent, which again made her want him to put his hands on her, to touch her…intimately.

"Yes," Serena said as she took a step toward the chair facing his desk. He'd not yet invited her to sit down, so she waited beside the chair.

Her gaze met his. He appeared to be six or eight years older than she was; in his late twenties or early thirties, she estimated. Impeccably dressed in a stylish suit, silk embossed grey tie, and elegant black John Lobb loafers. Even behind the European-cut black suit that was made of expensive material that flowed gently down his tall lean frame, she could tell he was in top physical shape with broad shoulders, muscular arms and a ripple, hard torso. Not at all typical of a professor. His rock star thick lips, pressed into a tight line of discontent, still showed their potential for being soft and sensuous. Serena's eyes, too embarrassed to look at him in the eye, was riveted to his lips, which looked more and more enticing as she imagined what he could do with them against her skin.

"Have a seat," he said with a curt nod to the chair.

Setting her handbag on the floor, she sat and placed her hands primly on her lap.

"I take it you're looking for an adviser." He opened the folder on his desk and perused the documents.

"Yes. Exactly. I'm finishing my…"

"How are your grades?" He held a sheet of paper up to examine it.

Caught off guard by the blunt question, she hesitated. "Um, good. I mean great. My average is…"

"And I assume you'd like to graduate next year." With finality, he set the documents back into the folder and shut it.

"Um, yes. That's true. I've been here three years and…"

"Well," he said as he put his hands on top of his desk and stood. "Unfortunately that's all the time we have."

"What? But I just got here. We haven't even discussed…"

"Rules are rules."

"What do you mean?"

"Miss Singleton. I don't know how you've managed to get by these past years – perhaps you've been lucky enough to have rather tolerant and indulgent professors – but I do not appreciate tardiness. You were not a mere five minutes or even ten minutes late, Miss Singleton. You, with all your high aspirations of graduating a year early, arrived at my office a full twenty minutes late."

"But I arrived at the school on time. I left home early and…it's only when I got here that I couldn't find parking. The student parking lot where I usually park is never this full and I didn't expect the administrator's lot… I had to drive around a dozen times before I finally spotted someone… and I'm wearing these tight shoes and the heels… and my skirt…"

"I have no desire to hear your excuses, Miss Singleton, though you appear to have many. What I do have, however, is another student who is about to knock on that door… any moment now."

"No." Horrified, she stood up to look straight at him. "I need you. I have to have an advisor, or else I'll…"

"You should have thought of that earlier, Miss Singleton."

"You can't shoot me down because I underestimated how cramped your little parking lot would be."

"Insults will get you nowhere, Miss Singleton."

"Please." With tears in her eyes, she reached down for her handbag, set it on the chair and pulled out a tissue. "I have to have an advisor. Please Professor, um. Shoot, I know your name, but I can't even think, you got me so flustered…" She knocked over her bag, spilling the content onto the floor.

"I'm sorry…I…" she bent down to pick up some of her content…a hairbrush, a pack of chewing gum, a pen, and… She gulped. A pack of edible underwear still in its packaging.

Serena turned a bright red as she realized what that was doing in her bag. It must have been in the nice designer handbag she borrowed from her best friend Laura, for this meeting. Laura was pretty adventurous and proud to let everyone know about it. Hopefully this professor didn't see it.

She looked up into his intense blue eyes, whose disdainful expression hadn't changed from before. Thank goodness he didn't see that. What must he think of her as a potential student, if she was caught with those on her. She quickly put all the spilled content out back into her bag, while she got up off her knees, trying to avoid looking clumsy while his blue eyes swept over her body from head to toe, lingering a while on her face and breast. "I'm so sorry, Professor Williamson. I'm not usually this flustered or clumsy. I'm…"

He shot her a derisive snort. "Sorensen. Sebastian Sorensen."

"Professor Sorensen, please don't be so casual about my future. I'm an above average student and any one of my professors can attest…"

"Miss Singleton. I am not merely throwing you out of my office on principle. I do have other students to see, you understand, and…" He looked at his watch. "The next student, if they dare arrive on time, should be here in ninety seconds."

"Then, please reschedule me. I'll be here an hour early. I'll do whatever you want. Please, Professor, this is far too important to me. I can't just let go because of something as trivial as a few minutes of tardiness."

"I'm sorry, but the *trivial* matter of your tardiness is not my problem."

"Professor, I'm begging. I'll do anything. I'll clean your office, get your dry cleaning, walk your dog, help grade papers. Truly, I'll do anything to make up for offending you."

He sat back down and eyed her over his clasped hands. "I admit, I'm overloaded. I have more work than I can handle, but I can't receive any…"

"But it wouldn't be a bribe. I'd be working for you, just as if you'd hired me."

With a keen glint in his fair blue eyes, he scrutinized her, from the tightly pulled dark hair that retreated into her chignon, to the parting of her lips, to her primly covered but full breasts and down to tiny waist, slim hips, and her long shapely legs and leather clad feet.

"I don't know," he mused. "You're rather thin."

"Thin?" She looked down at herself. She'd always considered herself healthy and athletic, not thin. Besides, what did that have to do with anything?

"Maybe a little too thin."

"No," she said adamantly. "I'm not some frail damsel. I'm strong and capable, capable of whatever you have to throw at me."

"The thing is…" He eyed her intently. "If anything, I might need your help at my house, but…"

"I can cook. I can clean. I even do windows."

Amused, he chuckled. "You really do want an adviser."

"Yes, sir."

Showing more interest in her, he stood and came around the desk to stand before her. His gaze was steady and curious as he reached out to gently

16

wrap his fingers around her forearm. "Very petite. Thin…"

"I prefer the word, 'slender'," Serena said quickly. "What exactly do you have in mind? What am I so petite for?" Though intrigued by him, she feared he could very well ask something of her that she could not do.

Releasing her arm, he walked around her, trailing his long but strong finger across her shoulder, sending a bolt of desire through her. "You're not too bad, though not quite the cool beauty Willow is."

"Willow?" Serena said, trying to hide the sting of his comment.

He waved her comment away. "All right, Miss Singleton, this is the situation. I have a family gathering I must attend. I also have an invitation to bring along a guest. I would like to avoid Willow and her gold-digging mother. I think if I had a young woman on my arm, a date, as it were, I could more easily avoid contact with them. At the very least, it would diminish their very ardent attempts at getting my attention."

17

Frowning, Serena stared straight ahead. This wasn't quite the deal she'd bargained for. "You want me to be your date?"

"What's the matter?" he said with an amused chuckle. "Is the notion that unappealing?"

She pulled her shoulders back and regained her composure. "No, not at all. I'm just a little surprised."

A gentle knock sounded at the door and the professor glanced at Serena then the doorknob. "What will it be?"

"If I accept, we will talk about my adviser situation, right?"

"Consider it done."

Serena shot a sidelong glance at the door as a firmer knock sounded.

"Yes," Professor Sorensen called out. "I'll be right with you." He looked expectantly at Serena, his blue eyes assessing her.

"Okay, I'll do it."

"Good. Meet me here in an hour... sharp, and we'll discuss a few details. We need to get a little acquainted before I introduce you to everyone."

"Yes, sir. Right. Of course, Professer Sorensen. Yes, thank you. You have no idea how..."

"I must meet with my next student," he said with a patient and tolerant tone.

"Yes, right. Absolutely." She fumbled to get her handbag and sling it over her shoulder then reached out to shake his hand.

He simply grinned and guided her to the door. "In an hour sharp."

Chapter 1

Sitting at her beat up, old upright Ludwig, Serena plunked her finger absentmindedly down the same key over and over again; middle C. Her eyes glued to the living room window that overlooked the boulevard below, she viewed and reviewed the past few hours. The afternoon had taken a turn she'd not anticipated and the decision she now faced left her puzzled and confused.

She'd already been accepted in the graduate music composition program she'd enrolled in. At least that was settled; one less thing to worry about. Now all that remained was finding the suitable adviser.

Sebastian Oliver Sorensen. She'd heard a lot about the handsome and sexy professor, even met him shortly once before a long time ago. He was not so much a professor then, but more of a film composer. Still as sexy or even more so than before. The entire female student body spoke of his piercing blue eyes and sultry smooth voice that can convince any woman to peel off their clothes for him. For all the talk she'd heard about him, she still hadn't expected him to affect

20

her as he had. She forgotten how he was so young to be as accomplished as he was, and talk of his blue eyes and voice didn't even do him justice. She was sure that if he had been born in another time period, he would have been amongst the greats like Beethoven, Bach, and Mozart. Sebastian Sorensen was the modern equivalent of them. They were the rock stars of their times, and Sebastian was a rock star composer in modern times. *Just as sexy as one, too.* Serena could feel her face flush and nipples harden just thinking of Professor Sorensen's voice and presence.

As far as looks go, he was anointed by the gods. As far as talent, no one else can compare. He was where Serena hoped to be someday. A highly-sought after Oscar-winning film composer, a professor, and even a show producer.

"He'd be perfect as an adviser," she murmured as she spread her fingers over the keys and played a G chord. He was highly acclaimed in the music department and the musical community as well. He was in her chosen field and in the perfect position to help her. Though she mentally ran through the other possible candidates, no other professor at the university suited her needs the way Professor Sorensen did.

If only he hadn't made such an absurd request of her; escorting him to his family party. She was sure he can have his pick of women, so why her?

While the long fingers of her left hand stretched across the keys to settle on a C chord, she reached for her phone and set her elbow on a few keys causing an interesting, if not off key clamor. Glancing at the card the professor had given her, she punched in his number.

He answered too quickly, throwing her off.

"Um. Hello. Um, Professor Sorensen, this is Serena, Serena Singleton."

"So I see." His voice was warm velvet over the phone.

"I beg your pardon." Her foot tapped the piano's peddles in a nervous twitch.

"A little innovation they invented a while back: caller ID."

"Oh, yeah, right." She felt inexplicably flustered and was thankful he couldn't see her heated cheeks. "I'm sorry to bother you, but I was thinking about… I was thinking about the conversation we had."

"Good. I'm happy to see you're contemplating my invitation."

The low resonance of his voice held something sexy and sultry. Just by closing her eyes, she could see his smoldering gaze and the effect went directly to her lower belly.

"Well, the job… um, the invitation that you offered me… um, to be your escort for this family night you have, well…"

"Do I hear a note of uncertainty in your voice, Serena?"

She almost fell off the piano stool at the sound of her name. Raspy, gravelly, inflamed, her name had never sounded quite so appealing. This wasn't her. This giddy, clumsy and flustered girl wasn't the woman she was. She was cool, collected. She'd never been the kind of girl to swoon over a cute face, but…

Wiping the back of her forearm across her brow, she shot off the stool and headed to the window for some air.

Damn, why is it so hot in here?

"Well," she said after a moment to collect her thoughts, "it pains me to say this, because having you as an advisor is very important to me, but unfortunately, I must decline your offer."

"Really?" he said with an odd note of surprise.

"My answer is no. I cannot be your escort for the night."

"Funny," he said with an amused chuckle that bordered on derisive. "I thought you said you were desperate. If I remember correctly, you did say you'd do anything."

"I guess I'm not as desperate as I thought."

"Humph," he grunted. "And I guess I thought you were serious about wanting me as your adviser."

"No offense, Professor Sorensen, but I do have my reputation to consider. When I said I'd do anything, it was more in the order of walking your dog, running errands or cooking a meal. My intention was to compensate you for the time you had to sacrifice in order to reschedule my appointment. I wanted to repay you by saving you some time; make up the time you lost because of my tardiness. However, playing escort isn't really my thing. I've worked hard to have an academic career, to go back to college, and to get into the graduate program here. I'm serious about becoming a composer. I can't risk a blemish on my reputation by sleeping with my adviser, no matter how tempting. I'm surprised you'd risk your reputation by sleeping with a student."

He let out a loud and surprised, "Huh?"

"Sleeping with you would…"

"Sleep with me? Who said anything about sleeping with me?"

"You said you wanted me to be your escort for this party of yours."

"I said I wanted you to accompany me, yes, but that's all. If I implied differently, I apologize, but all I need is a dinner date."

Staring at the cars that sped by, Serena leaned her brow against the window pane. There was something almost insulting in the way he stressed his lack of desire to sleep with her.

"Look," he went on, "this is a public gathering and I don't want to go alone. I could always go with someone else, anyone else, but when you arrived and proposed doing anything for me, I thought… why not? You seemed willing enough to please, and it will give us a chance to talk so… Anyway, it's no big deal. I mean, it's probably just as well. Although you seem a little familiar, despite our brief little meeting, we don't really know each other and it could prove awkward."

Their little meeting had indeed been brief. Though Serena had been at his door an hour later as promised, the student in his office had been in no rush to leave him. By the time the love struck student walked out, there was barely ten minutes left before his next appointment. Being one of the most popular professors, and perhaps the most eligible bachelor in society with his many accomplishments, his family fortune, and looks; he was constantly bombarded with requests from everyone for his time. No wonder why he was strict with their meeting time. It wasn't personal. It couldn't be.

Other than a few minor and insignificant details, he knew nothing about her.

"I guess I should go with someone I know more thoroughly. I can always go through my list, but as it is, all the women I've dated or brought to events like these have always wanted to pursue a romantic relationship afterwards. You, on the other hand, just want me as an adviser. I'm glad to see you so serious about your music composition career. And you don't seem to have a clue about me, which I find refreshing, but can also be a small problem which my mother might find odd."

Tempted to let slip all she knew about him, she bit her bottom lip and smiled. Telling him she knew how sexually appealing every girl found him wouldn't help matters. Worse still was the possibility of accidentally hinting that she might be attracted to him as well.

"Too bad," Sebastian said. "I think you would have liked it, but look, I honestly won't have the time to interview you before two weeks from now. My agent and manager wonder why I'm even 'wasting' time teaching at an university instead of working fully in composition, but ever since last year, I felt compelled to help those starting out, like you. But still trying to balance the music career I have so forgive me for trying to make this dinner date into a get-to-know-you meeting, too. I'm putting a lot of hours into my new composition and I'll be flying out for business right after this fundraiser thing my parents are throwing."

"A fundraiser? A get-to-know-you-meeting?" Intrigued, Serena couldn't hide her sudden interest.

"You didn't tell me this was for a fundraiser. I love fundraisers. In that case, I'd love to help out."

A dry laugh rang through her phone. "Would you now? Well, now that I've piqued you interest, I may as well tell you that it's going to be on a yacht, a relatively small one, but a yacht all the same. It's at the Newport Harbor, and the food is supposed to be wonderful."

"Are you trying to convince me, Professor?"

"Don't read anything into this, but I thought you'd make good company; after all, if you're looking to have me as your advisor it must be in part due to your love of music, right? I think it could make for interesting conversations. At least we'd have that in common and that could make up for the lack of knowledge we have of one another."

A sense of bewilderment fluttered through her. She hadn't expected this type of declaration from him. He seemed more like the type who would want a woman on his arm simply for the physical gratification, not to actually converse with. And the fact he was teaching because he wanted to help mentor and bring up the new generation of music composers was admirable. With his awards and connections, he could easily spend his time hobnobbing with the rich and famous, writing compositions all day, and walking the red carpet; not hanging out with students. "Congratulations. You convinced me. I'd be happy to go."

"Good, I'm glad that's settled. We'll discuss the details later."

"Fine, then. I'll wait to hear from you." She cringed. That sounded way too eager.

"Oh, by the way, do you have something appropriate to wear?"

"Appropriate how?"

"Classy, elegant, something really nice."

She let out a tense snort. "Not really. Since starting school, I've been so focused on my studies…I only brought some ordinary day dresses and the clothes I wear to go to school. The nice stuff I have is in storage."

"Don't worry. I'll find something for you. I have to run down to pick up my tux so I could swing by and pick you up. I know a few places we can go and you'll find something appropriate in no time."

"A tux, huh?"

"Yeah, it's that kind of evening."

"I don't know. I don't think…"

"I saw in your file that you live off campus, but Harbor Boulevard isn't that far off my route."

"Thanks, I appreciate it, but I have a friend who has a pretty decent wardrobe, so I'll see what she can do for me."

"If that's what you prefer, fine, however, since I'm the one who asked you to come to this shindig, I would pay for the dress."

She laughed. "Oh, Lord, no. That'd only make matters worse."

"Why?"

"Because then I'd owe you one, Professor."

"All right," he said with a throaty laugh. "Have it your way. We'll talk again soon."

Chapter 2

"So you've finally met the notorious Professor Sorensen." Laura poured herself a glass of white wine and leaned over her kitchen counter to look at Serena. Her long tapered fingers tapped lightly on the glass, sending the aromatic liquid quivering.

"I have to admit, he is a pretty good looking man." Having declined a glass of wine, Serena sipped her mineral water, though a nervous twitch in her gut beckoned for a single sip of alcohol.

"Good looking? My God, Serena, he's gorgeous, at least that's what I've heard. I haven't had the pleasure of meeting him yet." Laura eyed Serena with disbelief. "No one on campus can understand what he's doing behind the scenes writing music when he could easily be in front of the camera wooing millions. I mean, the world is his oyster, but all he wants to do is shuck."

"Not everyone in California wants to be a celebrity, Laura. Some actually take their craft seriously. This is a man who lives for his music. I think composing beautiful music is a noble endeavor."

"Yeah. You would."

"You gotta follow your passion in life. Music is what he loves. I can totally understand that."

Laura took a good swallow. "Listening to you, you'd think you could see straight through to his soul."

"It's not that hard to figure out. He loves music and wants to share that love with his students. I'm sure that's why he's here at Irvine instead of traveling the world wooing millions."

"Either way, I'm sure tonight is going to turn out to be quite the eye opener. Do you even realize how lucky you are? If the girls at Irvine get wind of this, they'll want your hide."

"That's encouraging."

"Hey, somebody's got to win over that adorable professor. There's no point letting all that talent go to waste."

Serena knew exactly what Laura meant by 'talent'. "Just because the guy is good looking and single doesn't mean he's going to waste. Besides, I'm hardly going to 'win over' Professor Sorensen. It's a platonic date. I'm just doing him a favor."

"Look, however you want to call it, you're still damn lucky."

"I completely agree, but not for the reasons you think. I'm lucky because after tonight I'll have him as my advisor and my success in the music composition program is pretty much guaranteed. Soon after that I'll be composing beautiful music just like him. I'll be his protégé, and the world better watch out!"

Laura winked. "And have wild hot sex with him at the same time. That's what every girl around Professor Sorensen wants." She smiled. "And every guy wants to have what he has...hung like a horse, I hear."

"Oh, get your head out of the gutter for a minute."

Laura closed her eyes. "Hmm, Professor Sorensen, sexy voice, bedroom eyes, sultry lips, body built for non-stop fucking..." She opened her eyes and looked at Serena. "Nope. Just the thought of him and my mind goes straight to the gutter. What can I say? Some guys just have that effect on people."

"Well, he doesn't have that effect on me."

Laura picked up her glass of wine and led the way to her bedroom. "Still, we can try to make it so

33

you have that same effect on him. I think I know the perfect dress for you."

"The idea isn't to wow him with…"

"With what? That hot little body of yours? If I wasn't straight, I'd be tempted. Slender everywhere except for your God-given large round boobs and butt? God, what women would kill to have b & b (boobs and butt) like yours. The only way would be through surgery, girl, and I say…if you've got it, flaunt it."

Serena rolled her eyes up. "I just don't want anything too revealing. Nothing too sleazy, Laura. This is a fundraiser; a family fundraiser at that. I don't want his mom to see me and think I'm just another tramp.

"Honey," Laura said with a dramatic pout. "You're hurting my feelings."

"I didn't mean to imply that your wardrobe is sleazy, though you have to admit you do own a few questionable items."

The dramatic pout quickly turned into a wicked grin. "Being a little naughty from time to time never hurt anyone. At least I have sex often."

Serena frowned. Having sex often wasn't something she would be proud to admit. Where she was from as a child, women had it all the time, only it wasn't a badge of triumph, but a way to make a living, often with a steep price to pay.

"Laura, honey, you know me…it's the quality of the sex, not the quantity."

"And Professor Sorensen definitely counts as quality and quantity at the same time, if you can even get him interested in you like that. I heard girls and women (way older than him even) throw themselves shamelessly at him. Whether he indulges is another thing. I heard he's insatiable. Well-built and satisfying, too. Never leaves a woman unsatisfied and not thoroughly fucked." Laura closed her eyes in reverence. "God what a man."

"I'm to be his protégé, Laura," Serena said. "Hopefully, if he's my adviser, I can get half as talented as he is in music composition."

"Either way, darling, you are going to look ravishing."

With flair she pulled out a pretty lace hanger on which hung a shimmering gown of gold. "With your dark hair, I think this would look great on you. It'll also enhance that sun kissed glow of yours and will make your large green eyes pop."

35

Serena looked at the garment with a touch of distaste. "I don't know." She fingered the thin straps that ran down to the low cut back.

"The hanger doesn't do it justice. Just try it on then decide."

"Fine." Unconvinced, Serena took the hanger and headed to the bathroom. The fabric felt expensive and when she saw the designer's name, she gasped. How on earth could Laura lend her such a dress? It most likely cost more than her rent. Emerging a few moments later, she remained pessimistic.

"Why the glum face, gorgeous?"

"I'm just not sure, Laura. I feel… too exposed."

"Have you seen yourself?" Laura took Serena by the elbow and led her to the full length mirror beside the closet door. "Look at that and tell me you don't look like a beautiful golden goddess."

Serena tilted her head to the side as she took in her reflection. It did fit her perfectly and the effect wasn't as gaudy as she'd anticipated. It clung to all the right places, emphasizing her breasts, slender waist, and curves, while flowing softly down to highlight her long shapely legs.

"And," Laura said as she came behind her and pulled her hair up, "look how elegant that looks. A touch of mascara, some light blush on your incredible high cheekbones, a soft lipstick and you're set."

Smiling, Serena could now see the full picture coming together. Though daring, the dress was elegant and classy. "Okay, I'll take it."

"Great." Laura opened the closet door and pulled out golden four inch slingbacks. "And take these."

Serena slipped her feet in.

"From sweaty sweats to refined goddess." Laura applauded. "I don't think I've ever seen you look quite so beautiful and fuckable."

"Laura!" Serena scolded. "That's not..."

Laura laughed. "Having sex appeal isn't a bad thing, girl. You have it, don't hide it. You can go back to sweats and college grad garb afterwards. Enjoy tonight as a desirable woman on the arm of the hot and sexy Sebastian Sorensen."

Chapter 3

Sebastian whistled a frivolous tune as he drove his Roadster out of Newport Beach's Fashion Island's parking lot. The newly tailored Armani suit he'd picked up fit him perfectly and going to his mother's bash that night seemed a little more palatable.

Out of curiosity, he passed in front of the address he'd seen in Serena's file. Not bad, he thought. Nothing like the penthouse suite he had in the imposing glass and steel towers that faced the ocean, but still... not bad.

Grinning at the last minute arrangement he'd made for the night, he drove on as he mentally dressed Serena. Would she go for something somber, even matronly, or would she play it stylish and classic? Truth was he wondered what she'd look like in something a little slinky... a little sexy. She had potential for sure, with what little he saw. Was that a package of edible underwear he thought that fell out of her bag? He couldn't help but smile. If so, there was more to Serena Singleton than his first impression of her.

She was thin; a little too thin for his liking, but with a few extra pounds, he felt certain she'd have interesting and tantalizing curves…like her breasts that seemed to strain against her prim and proper blouse. And her pouty lips…lips that looked as sweet as candy. The tight pencil skirt she'd worn that morning which hugged her bottom like a glove, had hinted at many possibilities he'd like to explore with his hands, though something innocent, even naïve had made it clear she had no idea the potential she had. That in itself made her a little intriguing and enticing. A woman who doesn't know her own potential for passion. How he'd like to open that up within her, get her to tap into that, and make something great out of her. He can already see the potential she had as one of his students. Now if he can get through all those layers of clothing, insecurities, and emotional barriers; he could help her break out of her shell and possibly inspired her to be a great composer. Already she had been a challenge, being late to their meeting like that and insisting he drop everything to meet with her. How presumptuous. How rebellious. How much she deserves to be taught a lesson on being punctual. He would gladly give her a good spanking to show her that kind of behavior cannot be tolerated, and such a prim and proper outfit would stifle anyone's creativity.

Something about her seemed familiar and strangely erotic, though, despite her harsh student outfit. She would definitely be a challenge…a challenge he'd be drawn to take.

He parked his car in the underground parking lot, draped his new suit over his arm and took the elevator to his suite. The moment he set foot in his home, he was once again reminded of his mother's taste for everything refined. It was no wonder. She'd insisted he use her good friend Olivia Winston to decorate the suite while he'd insisted he wanted a décor that suited his personality, not hers.

Though he would have preferred a younger and more avant-garde designer, he'd called Olivia. She'd been eager to meet with him; too eager. While Sebastian had anticipated the move she'd make on him, he hadn't quite expected her to be so persistent. On more than one occasion, he'd had to physically pry her off him, something that revolted him.

The Protégé by Kailin Gow

In her mid-forties, Olivia was a beautiful woman who knew it all too well. The more he'd come to know her, the more her beauty had been marred by her vanity. She had a body many twenty year olds would envy, but she was far from what Sebastian had in mind as a lover. Her aggressive nature turned him off and he'd taken to avoiding her whenever possible. Fundraisers such as the ones his mother had planned made it virtually impossible.

As he set his suit on the bed, he had to admit Olivia had at least proven to be talented as far as décor was concerned. Between attempts to get into his bed, she'd managed to do a decent job. His room was elegant yet simple and masculine. The neutral colors, taupe, black and brown, suited his mood. The heavy oak furniture lacked the flourished carvings his mother was so fond of. It was streamlined and simple, just as he liked it.

After a quick glance at the clock on his bedside table, he hurried into the shower. He would have preferred a long lingering shower, the kind that erased the pressures of the day; the kind that left his mind roaming to new melodies, new harmonies and breathtaking crescendos. Instead, he lathered up and rinsed off in record time.

Patting his skin dry, he gazed in the mirror. He looked decent, he thought, though his mother would probably remind him again of his need to get a haircut. She'd never understood why he'd allowed his hair to flow down to his shoulders. As he turned to look sidelong at his reflection, he could easily see the arrogant gleam in his eye; the one that'd left him with a reputation for being as arrogant as he looked. Shrugging off the opinion of those he cared little for, he shaved and slapped on a little after shave. This was a large-scale fundraiser after all.

Back in his bedroom he slowly and meticulously put on the articles of clothing that made up the elegant suit he'd chosen. Standing tall and proud, he admired his reflection in the mirror and once again thought of Serena.

How would she look on his arm?

As they'd stood face to face in his office, he'd noticed her height. With heels she'd almost be eye to eye with him. Would she wear her long hair up? Or would it be wild and flowing?

Judging from the way she looked today in his office, bedraggled, uptight, and plainly dressed; he wasn't sure if she was the right choice. Could she pull off looking like someone everyone expected him to be dating, versus the coolly beautiful Willow? Either way, he just hoped he wouldn't regret bringing someone so simple and plain spoken to such an elegant soiree. As sweet and innocent as she was, she could easily be swallowed up by the cougars, prowlers and vipers who so deceptively dressed in satin and silk, and dripped with rubies and diamonds.

Then again, Serena did prove to have complete disregard for rules. She had no concept of the order of things. Maybe she'd be the one showing those old cougars a thing or two. He laughed as he hustled to the kitchen and grabbed his car keys. Serena had dared refuse him. Perhaps she had more bite than she let on.

Out of the corner of his eye he spotted the vase filled with luscious red roses.

Perfect, he thought as he reached out to pluck one out.

"Thanks, Becky," he said. His housekeeper insisted on bringing in fresh flowers and while he'd often found them frivolous, he had to admit they added something warm to his home. And tonight, one would add a touch of romance to this last minute dating arrangement.

The bad mood that'd sat on his shoulders since receiving his mother's invitation slowly dissipated as he took the elevator back down to the parking lot. He realized now that far beyond the annoyance of his mother's constant stream of fundraisers, luncheons, banquets and balls, it was the company she kept that truly grated his nerves.

Olivia would be there and she'd used every seductive tactic in the book to try to get into his pants. Other mothers in attendance would try to set him up with their daughters; aunts with their nieces. He knew being a bachelor left him open to so many advances, but he wished everyone would just understand his need to be free of any entanglements at the moment. He had his career to think about and his lifestyle. He enjoyed getting and receiving sexual gratification from partners mutually seeking a purely physical relationship like that, and he wasn't about to give that up to be tied down in matrimony to a woman like Willow or Olivia.

Getting into his Roadster, he felt that need for freedom. The leather seat hugged him without suffocating him. The steering wheel yielded to his every command without complaint. The stick shift maneuvered the car as he willed it and didn't argue. And… the motor purred, not whined.

A willing body to have sex with; that was easy. Eager students, faculty members, starry-eyed young singers who performed in his musicals; they all wanted him. They all wanted a part of him. They all wanted the possibilities he could offer them; advancement in their career. Something from him, even pure sexual pleasure. Sometimes he was willing to give it, but since a year ago when he stumbled into a situation where it almost ended badly, he had been more careful. He never ever wanted to hurt anyone, feelings or physically. It was a line he would never cross and felt strongly other men should never cross, too.

He put the car into gear and gunned it once he reached the freeway. His eagerness to see Serena suddenly sent a shot of blood rushing between his thighs. Just curious, he said to himself. That tight pencil skirt and buttoned up shirt had been a severe way of hiding the woman she was. And that hair. He laughed as the image of her came to his mind. Who wore such a tight and demure chignon these days? Not

45

even his mother. What was Serena hiding? Was she hiding anything at all or she simply had a wall built up to shelter her from getting hurt. Who had hurt her before where she would withdraw into herself like that?

"Now let's see what you're really made of, Miss Singleton."

Chapter 4

Sebastian parked his car in the underground garage and took the elevator to the twelfth floor. The fact that she lived in an apartment complex that was not typically occupied by students was a relief. Though he wasn't officially dating her, he still didn't want any misunderstanding to compromise his reputation at the university.

As the elevator doors slid open, he let out a long, low whistle. "Pretty impressive for a mere student."

Though not as opulent as the building he lived in, it was nonetheless tastefully decorated and offered an aura of tranquility with a dash of luxury.

The carpeting was obviously new, still plush and thick. The walls boasted a handsome grouping of paintings, a few of which he could easily envision in his own home. Serena Singleton had exquisite taste, unlike many graduate students and women he'd known.

As meek and mild as Serena had seemed, she obviously had her life more in order than many young women her age. This building was not the typical starving student abode. Perhaps over the course of the evening he'd find out how she managed to afford living in such a building. Rich parents, or maybe several roommates.

With his rose held up before him, he brought his finger to the doorbell, but before he could even ring, the door open.

"Hello, Professor."

For a speechless moment, he stared at her, his blood rushing downward to the part of his body that was suddenly hardening. If there was ever a dress that can be an aphrodisiac, the one Serena was wearing now, had to be it. He wanted to grab her, flip up her dress, and take her from behind while grabbing her beautiful hand-filling breasts with both hands as leverage. The image of this, made him catch his breath. It was so sudden and unexpected, hitting him like a brick. He had to have this woman whether tonight or tomorrow, but his mind and dick won't rest until he knows how it feels to be in her and to hear her moan out his name in pure ecstasy.

"Professor?"

Sebastian licked his lips, backed up, looked down toward one end of the hall then the other. He looked up at the number beside her door and looked back at her. "I think I must have the wrong place," he joked, trying to regain his composure.

Serena let out a tickled giggle. "It's me, Professor."

"Please." He slapped his palm to his forehead. "Stop calling me Professor, Serena. We're going to dinner, and we have to at least act like we know each other. It's Sebastian… at least for tonight."

"Fine, Sebastian. Is that for me?" Serena asked as she reached out for the single rose.

"No," he said as he pulled it out of her reach. "It's for my mom."

A lovely flush of pink colored her cheeks as she held her hand aloft. "Oh."

"You're as gullible as you are lovely." He handed her the rose. "Of course, it's for you."

Taking the rose, she gave a megawatt smile that lit up her entire face, making her radiant and almost ethereally beautiful. Sebastian was speechless for a second time. What was going on? No one's ever

49

affected him this way before, especially not a student who was seeking him out as an adviser. He'd better put a lid on this lustful attraction or he'd really start to care about people and entanglements.

"I admit a part of me regretted our impromptu date." Sebastian's gaze roamed over her shoulders and dipped down into the curve of her waist and lingered on her breasts and cleavage before returning to her face. "I mean, you arrived at my office so… well, you looked like something the cat wouldn't even bother dragging in."

"Well gee, thank you, Prof… Sebastian. I needed that little pick me up. Now I feel so much better about myself." Serena made a face.

"Well, here comes the pick me up. You clean up like no other woman I've ever seen before." Sebastian licked his lips. "You're quite lovely, exquisitely beautiful even…why I haven't noticed that lovely green shade of your eyes before…"

"Yeah," Serena said, completely unmoved by the compliment. "Well, considering how low I apparently scored on our first meeting, seems I had a lot of room for improvement." After an awkward moment of silence, she added, "You clean up pretty nice, too."

Careful not to ogle, Sebastian took in the shimmering garment that clung to every gentle curve of her body. He'd barely heard a word she'd said as he took in every delicious inch of her. His hot eyes ignited her body, and he can see her get aroused, her nipples hardening under her thin gown. She'd opted to wear her long, dark hair free and flowing, and the effect was captivating. Shining like silk, the soft waves offered brilliant glimpses of copper. Her lips, glossed and luscious, beckoned him and he deeply regretted the boorish party that awaited them. At this very moment, he'd have easily accepted her invitation to sip a quiet glass of wine with her or better yet, from her body as he would pour wine into her navel and sip from it, as they became better acquainted.

He leaned in close... closer. Her perfume was delicate and sweet. He licked his lips, wanting to touch his hot tongue on her skin, his burning lips to hers.

"You like the dress I found?" Serena backed away, smiling as her eyes widened with surprise.

"Um, yes. Very… suitable. Your friend has lovely taste." She'd refused him, he noted.

"Yeah, and great shoes, too." She pinched the skirt of her gown and jacked it up a few inches to show her feet.

The sparkling gem-encrusted sandals could have looked gaudy, and probably would have on anyone else, but they looked stylish and perfect under Serena's toned and tanned legs, legs he'd like to run his hands over inch by delicious inch, and inner thighs he'd like to nibble and lick his way over to more intimate areas.

"You're going to give the ladies quite a run for their money with those, and your legs."

"I'm happy you like it. I admit, I initially regretted our little impromptu date, too. The moment I left your office, I was like, what did I get myself into? But, well, I think all this dressing up could be fun."

Sebastian offered his arm. Yes, fun. "Then, shall we?"

She slipped her hand into the crook of his arm and the mere touch of her hand against his sent an unexpected thrill through him, making him harder. "I think I'm going to enjoy this evening far more than I'd anticipated."

"Me, too," Serena said with a smile.

Chapter 5

With an expert hand, Sebastian drove the Roadster toward the coast. Serena's apprehension and uncertainty quickly gave way to a surprisingly serene sense of calm and belonging as Sebastian eased the car out of Costa Mesa then out of traffic and onto the scenic road that led to the dock.

Serena gazed out at the Pacific. The setting sun painted a glorious picture and she wondered if she'd ever tire of the beautiful sunsets the California coast offered. She turned and brought her attention back to Sebastian. He wasn't half bad to look at either. "Where d'you learn to drive like that?" she asked.

"Like what?" he said with a pleased and boyish grin.

"You drive fast, almost dangerously so, yet there's something smooth and sleek in every move you make. I feel like you're in complete control at all times."

"That I am." He shot her a knowing glance. "Actually, I learned to drive in Switzerland. Plenty of curves to keep a boy happy." He smiled wickedly.

"You lived in Switzerland?"

"Born there."

"Oh, I thought I'd noticed a slight accent when we first met. I couldn't quite put my finger on what it was. I thought perhaps German or something."

"It's barely discernable these days. My years in America have erased much of it, or so I'm told."

In the distance the shimmering lights of the dock came into view. As they got closer, Serena wondered which of the spectacular crafts they would board. They were all magnificent and impressive.

"Ready?" Sebastian said as he parked the car and killed the engine.

"As I'll ever be."

He came around the car and opened the door. Serena accepted the hand he offered and was caught off guard as his touch sent electric sparks running through her body. Quickly, she reminded herself of the role she was to play. This was to be a mere charade and her body had to keep that in mind. She'd have to play along while keeping any true emotion from entering the game.

When he tightened his hold of her, she leaned into him, letting herself become completely immersed in her role. She had to convince everyone they were actually dating; actually knew one another. It wasn't too difficult to fake. His body, muscular and strong, was like a magnet that was hard to pull away from. Her body was in perfect sync to his and she was surprised by how comfortable she felt at his side.

With a carriage worthy of the most notable prince, Sebastian led her to an extravagant multi-million dollar yacht. The moment they boarded, Serena was surrounded by everything that was rich and ostentatious.

"How many people work just to keep this thing glittering?" Her gaze darted from the glistening floors to the shinning rails to the glowing golden trim.

"We have a great crew," he said simply. "Come on. I'll show you around."

The guests in attendance were as impressive as the craft they'd boarded. Silks, sequins, crystals and diamonds; every single guest flaunted their wealth. Serena was eternally grateful she had a fashionable friend like Laura. Without her she'd have stuck out like a sore thumb.

Having grown up in Newport, Laura was the daughter of the founder of a successful chain of health food stores and had learned at a young age how to hold her own among the most affluent. With her auburn hair and fair skin, she would have fit right in with this crowd. Laura, as down to earth as she could be at times, had the innate ability to hold herself with a haughty air when the occasion suited her, along with her no-holds bar colorful language and rebelliousness.

As cultured and sophisticated as Serena now appeared, she'd had to learn the airs and ways of the wealthy. She'd done so, years ago to please him.

A soft and gentle smile came to tickle her lips as she thought of him; her ex, her first... He'd been the first man to make love to her. At nineteen she'd been innocent and considerably naïve when she'd met the twenty-nine year old man who'd swept her off her feet.

Not only had he introduced her to the pleasures of being a woman, he'd opened a whole new world of money, class and sophistication. He would have fit in perfectly with the crowd that now surrounded her.

Amused and feeling a little nostalgic, she peered through the crowd, hoping to perhaps spot him. Her eyes darted to every tall blond man in attendance, but none of them had his sparkling blue eyes. Nor did they have the exquisitely sexy body that had taught her so many lessons in love.

She allowed herself a moment to wonder what her view of men would be had it not been for the things she'd learned during that time. Would she still be as innocent and virginal as she'd been?

Enough indulging in the past, she thought with a mental shake of her head. That was over a couple of years ago… a lifetime ago. If anything, she'd put great effort into forgetting everything about him. She'd even gone so far as to avoid dating anyone who remotely resembled him. The men she'd known since had been dark and brooding. Less experienced, men she can easily dominate. They'd also been more down to earth which had come to suit her student status and lifestyle.

Her music career was what counted now, not pleasing a man.

Bringing her thoughts back to the present she took in the luxury that now enveloped her, feeling a bit more at home. The urge to let out an impressed whistle became stronger with every step, but Serena resisted and simply took in her beautiful surroundings with a restrained but appreciative nod.

"Hey, you okay?" Sebastian asked.

Serena looked up at him and realized how far away her thoughts had taken her. "Just a lot of memories. There was a time when I attended a lot of functions like this."

"Oh?" He smiled in appreciation. "You are indeed a fascinating and mysterious young woman. Hardly what I expected considering the disheveled kitten who walked into my office."

She waved the notion and conversation away. "It was a long time ago, and I've changed since then. My focus is on my music now. I want to concentrate on being a good student... the best, and I want to channel all my energy into my career as a composer."

His gaze was intense and solemn as Sebastian listened to her. "I look forward to discussing your ambitions."

"But for now..." she finished for him.

"Yes, for now we have guests to mingle with."

They strolled through the crowd, quickly greeting a variety of people. While many were young and attractive, the vast majority of them were older. Sophistication dripped from their fingertips and peering down over their noses seemed to be the norm.

"Do you spend a lot of time on this boat?" Serena asked as Sebastian led her to a quiet corner of the room.

Sebastian let out a soft little laugh. "Please don't let anyone hear you calling this a boat, my mother in particular. She'd have a conniption."

"Sorry, right. Do you spend a lot of time on this yacht?"

"Not as much as I'd like to. Sometimes I'd just like to take it out and get away from it all, but my schedule doesn't often permit it."

"It certainly seems to be the kind of place that could inspire beautiful music."

Nodding he led her outside. The salty evening air caressed her cheeks and she closed her eyes a moment, letting the breeze fan her hair.

"Here at the dock and filled with the most affluent residents of Southern California the atmosphere is almost cold and biting. It's not the most conducive atmosphere to write music. I'm sure you've already noticed how formal and forced everyone seems."

Serena nodded. She had noticed a few creased brows, tense smiles and practiced laughter as they'd made their way through the crowd. While they'd greeted Sebastian with respect, they'd barely glanced at Serena.

He pointed out toward the horizon. "Being out there, miles from shore all alone is quite another experience. It's breathtaking. Replenishing. Maybe I'll take you out some time." He leaned over the rail and looked out to the sea.

The sun still held remnants of deep dark gold as a last sliver peeked over the horizon.

"It's easy to understand," Serena whispered, feeling the freedom and tranquility Sebastian also felt at the moment. "Just looking out from here is magical."

"Come on," he said as he turned and gently took her by the arm, his eyes softening as he looked into hers. "We'd better meet and greet a few more people before my mother reprimands me for being so inhospitable."

"And where is your mother?"

Guiding her toward a pleasant looking older couple, Sebastian chuckled. "Don't worry. She's here somewhere. You'll meet her soon enough."

"Sebastian," the older man said.

"Doctor Howard." Sebastian nodded at the man then took the woman's hand to kiss her fingers. "Mrs. Howard. So pleased to see you could make it."

"You know how we love to support your mother and her fundraisers." Mrs. Howard said. "In particular this organization. The children's hospital does such phenomenal work and we know the money raised tonight will make such a difference in so many children's lives."

"Indeed." Sebastian brought Serena to the forefront. "If I may, I'd like to introduce you to Serena."

"A pleasure," the older woman said.

"Likewise," the man added.

"Are you involved with the fundraiser?" Mrs. Howard asked.

"Bash!" A booming female voice called out before Serena could answer.

Sebastian closed his eyes and Serena saw a light hint of tension spread across his jaw line.

"Bash, it's about time you got here." An attractive elegant older woman draped in colorful chiffon intruded the quiet foursome. Her bright blue eyes quickly took in Serena's dress before turning to Sebastian. "How long have you been here? Why didn't you come see me right away?"

"I arrived just a few moments ago, Mother. I've barely had time to make the rounds and I felt it imperative to greet the good doctor and his lovely wife." He leaned in closer to his mother. "You know how Father can be about these things."

After a nod of salutation, the good doctor and his lovely wife quietly walked away.

"So happy you came," Mrs. Sorensen called out after them. The moment they were out of earshot she turned to Sebastian. "Can you believe that dress she's wearing? I feel like it's 1996 all over again."

"I thought she looked lovely, Mother."

"Yes, well, you were always a little behind the times."

Serena cocked a brow, surprised by the woman's open reprimand of her adult son.

63

"And on a cheerier note, Mother, this is Serena Singleton."

Mrs. Sorensen offered Serena three feeble and limp fingers in lieu of a handshake.

"Pleased to meet you, Mrs. Sorensen."

"Yes. Yes." The woman made no attempt to hide her discontent. "Sebastian, you do know that Willow Brooks and her mother have arrived, don't you?"

"No. I'd not seen them yet, Mother."

"Well, it's high time you did. Willow is positively ravishing tonight. I hardly doubt a man here will be able to keep his eyes off her all night."

"Yes," Sebastian said with a sheepish glance at Serena. "It wouldn't be the first time."

"Come on, then. Let's go greet them before they get the impression you're deliberately trying to avoid them." She slipped her hand into the crook of his arm. "Besides, they've just returned from that fabulous cruise on the Rhine and I'm sure they'll have plenty to talk about."

"Mother, this is the first time Serena is on our yacht and…"

"No excuses, son. This family has a reputation to uphold and I won't have you tarnishing it by snubbing a family such as the Brooks."

With that, she tugged on his arm and led him away.

Serena took a few steps in an attempt to follow them, but was quickly swallowed up by the elitist crowd. Just as well, she thought. Mrs. Sorensen gave the distinct impression she wanted her son all to herself. Though she'd promised herself she wouldn't get emotional about her night with Sebastian, she couldn't help but feel a sting of jealousy as he and his mother greeted a beautiful tall blond wearing a decidedly plunging white gown.

"You look a little lost."

Serena turned to face a tall and handsome young man who looked intently at her.

"Lovely, but lost," he added.

Staring at him, Serena tried to remember if they'd already been introduced. She'd seen so many faces and had heard so many names. No, she thought. She'd surely remember such a face. Boyish and charming, he had big puppy-dog blue eyes, a comical grin and wavy brown hair that beckoned fingers to run through it.

"I'm Michael," he offered as he reached for her hand. "Looks like I got the better end of the deal."

"Serena, Serena Singleton." She tilted her head in confusion. "What 'better end'?"

His kissed her fingers, letting his lips linger a warm moment before releasing her.

"Well, I'm here with you instead of over there with my gold digging sister and overbearing mother."

How quaint, she thought.

"I don't believe I've ever seen you at one of these functions before. I'm certain I would remember such a face."

"You're absolutely right. This is the first time coming to one of Mrs. Sorensen's fundraisers."

"Invited by Mrs. Sorensen herself?"

"No. I'm here with Mr. Sorensen."

Michael frowned with confusion.

Serena felt a heated blush come to her face and cursed her faux pas. "Sebastian Sorensen."

"Ah, yes. The famed musical composer. I never thought composing bland and dreary music could appeal to so many women. Then again, I'm sure the Sorensen fortune has something to do with it."

"I happen to love the music Sebastian composes."

"A fan, huh?"

"If you want to call it that."

Michael looked past her and smirked. Serena turned to see Sebastian surrounded by three blonds. His mother, the tall and exquisite Willow, and another older woman, Willow's mother, who seemed to have a constant sour expression glued to her face.

"I think my sister is going to keep your date busy for quite a while." He'd put a question mark on the word date. With his strong hand at the small of her back, he gently led her away. "Given that you don't know anyone else here, I believe that leaves me with the obligation to keep you company and show you around."

His smile was heated and intense as Serena followed his lead. "Funny," he said as he guided her to the upper deck. "I'd quite expected this evening to be a dud; a snore; a bore."

"That's not very nice."

"People who have tons of money sometimes lose all sense of fun. Their idea of fun is arguing whether they're drinking a Chardonnay or Merlot. To make things really exciting they might throw in a Bordeaux or Chianti."

"You certainly have an odd opinion of your own…" She caught herself and stopped.

"What? An odd opinion of my own kind?" His smile was warm and teasing.

As a waiter slowly passed by balancing a tray laden with flutes of champagne, Michael grabbed two and handed one to Serena.

With a smile, she nodded her thanks and took a sip. "Well, sort of."

"Look, every time I come to one of these things, I see people who put all their efforts into being elegant and classy; showing off basically. And, of course, they get a kick out of putting down all those who don't live up to their high standards. It gets dull and dreary pretty fast."

"And you're not one of those people who like to show off?" she chided. "Come on. How many times have you picked up a lovely young woman with a flashy and showy car? How many times have you tried to dazzle a woman with expensive jewelry or a night out at an exclusive restaurant?"

He laughed, a hearty and pleased sound that came from deep within. "Touché. Guilty as charged. But..." He held up an explanatory finger. "I still know how to have fun. I mean, if I invite you on a date, yes, I'll pick you up in my silver Mercedes, and after a few dates I'd surely want to show my affection for you by giving you a beautiful tennis bracelet or teardrop earrings. Throughout the process, however, I'll show you tons of fun."

"Really?" Serena said with mock disbelief. "And how does a boy raised in such luxury have fun these days?"

"The better question," he said as he peered over her shoulder. "Is what is a lovely and lively girl like you doing with Mr. Dark and Moody?"

"Is that really your opinion of Sebastian?" She glanced back to see Sebastian wading through the crowd as he tried to make his way towards them.

"Or Bash, as my sister loves to call him." He rolled his eyes on Bash. "She thinks that just because Mrs. Sorensen calls him that, she can too. It sounds so pathetic. But, to answer your question, yes. I mean, look at him."

Once again, Serena glanced over her shoulder.

"He is dark. He is moody. I mean, the hair, the music, the brooding. It's like he's trying to be some great 16th century genius. Like he wants to impersonate Mozart or something."

"And what do you know about classical music and the greats?"

He shrugged. "This movie I saw. Then again, I guess dark and moody is in these days. I mean my sister certainly didn't waste much time laying claim to him." After an awkward silence, he put his hand over his mouth. "Oops, sorry. I didn't mean to let that slip out."

"What?" Serena said with casual disinterest, though her heart raced for some inexplicable reason. "Have they been seriously seeing each other?"

"Well, I overheard Mother saying Willow had already picked out her wedding gown. A twenty-thousand dollar thing covered with crystals and all those things you girls like."

"That's a pleasant stereotype."

"Are you going to tell me you don't dream of that magical day? Princess?"

Serena tried to hide just how annoyed she was by everything he was saying; not only his idea of women and weddings, but the relationship between Sebastian and Willow.

"In a sense it's like they've been engaged since childhood," he went on. "At least that's what my mother and Mrs. Sorensen seemed to think; though Sebastian seems to like to play hard to get whenever he can. In time, I think he'll come around. I mean my sister might be a little coo coo sometimes, but, I guess in some circles, she's considered a catch."

"I think it's pretty obvious he's not interested in her at all. Otherwise, why would he have brought me here?"

He shrugged. "Dark and moody. I guess that also means he's hard to figure out. I've seen him go through all kinds of women over the years; tall ones, short ones, rich ones, poor ones; talented songstresses, serious businesswomen and artsy whack jobs. Of course he's had a healthy dose of models and starlets in there, too." He brought his fingers to her hair and played with a thick strand. "Sounds like you're a very decent girl, Miss Singleton, not the type to get caught up in all this lunacy. I would hate to see you get hurt by him, or by this little game my mother and Willow insist on playing."

"So you think this is all a game?"

"Hey, there you are." Sebastian came up behind Serena and immediately put a possessive hand around her waist. He glared at Michael and the tension between the two was instantly palpable.

Michael released the lock of hair he'd been fingering. "You should know better than to leave such a beautiful creature all alone."

"Were it not for your persistent sister, I never would have." He turned to Serena. "I didn't mean to abandon you like that. Mother can be rather insistent when she gets an idea in her head."

"So I noticed."

"Excuses, excuses," Michael said with an uninterested smirk. He nodded a salutation to Serena and shot one last glare at Sebastian. "Better keep her close... Mr. Sorensen. My time with her was all too short and I'll jump at the chance to accompany her again. She's a veritable breath of fresh air amidst all the stale blowholes here." He snickered. "And I love to see the effect she has on Willow and our conniving mothers. Bring her around more often." He walked away.

"Mr. Sorensen?" Sebastian wiped the disgusted expression off his face and turned to Serena. "What's that about?"

"Sorry. When he first asked who I'd come with… To me you're still the professor and…"

"You okay?" Sebastian said as he brushed away her slip up. "Michael is a notorious womanizer and I can just imagine the games he tried to play with you."

"I'm fine. He was very polite and a good company. Handsome and a true gentleman."

"Is that a crack at me?" Though his smile was genuine, a light frown furrowed his brow.

"Not at all. I understand these events require you to mix and mingle. You just can't expect me to stay glued to the wall as you do so."

He leaned an elbow on the rail and looked at her. His eyes darted from the windswept tendrils of hair, to her eyes and down to the glistening gold of her dress, and her cleavage. "He is right, though. I'd have to be crazy to leave you alone with all these sharks roving about."

"Well, I got a glimpse of this Willow person and I can certainly understand you."

With a sardonic chuckle he looked out at the darkening sea. "She's the epitome of the pretty bow on an empty package. She knows how to work her physical attributes to perfection, but she hasn't a clue how to tap into her own soul."

"That's a cold assessment."

"It's an accurate one."

"She can't be all that bad if she's so interested in you."

He turned a solemn gaze to her. "How about we talk about something else? Like you, maybe."

Looking at him, the words Michael had said about him rang in her head. "Michael seems to find it odd that I would be here with you. Seems you have an interesting history of womanizing yourself."

"You have to taste a variety of foods before you learn what you really like."

"No need to get defensive… Bash." The name sounded like a joke on her lips and she promised herself she'd never call him by the silly diminutive again. "A man with experience is far more interesting than a man who's never known a woman. Of course a woman still has the desire to feel special in a man's company, not like just another notch on his belt, but a colorful history can make a new relationship a little spicier."

"Hmmm," he mused with an impressed, but stunned cock of his brow. "I didn't really think you'd be the type..."

"The type of what? Woman who enjoys hands that know what they're doing? Lips that understand how to stoke a flame? Please... it's every woman's fantasy."

"Really?"

"Just like men fantasize about women who are either virginal or full on seductresses."

His smoldering gaze bore down to the heated folds between her thighs. Dark and moody, Michael had said. Yes, so perfectly dark and moody...and delicious. She had to admit it was part of his appeal, and she had to admit it was working. If he was like any of his music, he would be complex, explosive, sweet, sensual, and passionate. She wanted to get to know the man who could evoke such emotions in her just from

75

one part of her senses. What would it be like to have all of her senses ignited like that?

"And which one are you?" he asked, his voice huskier than before.

The sexy curve of his lips was more tantalizing than Serena had thought possible. They were full, sensual, and possessive. The kind you can spend hours nibbling on. It wasn't hard to imagine the softness of his lips over hers. And his hands... Every time he touched her she felt the intense heat that raced throughout her body.

She chuckled, a sexy sound that came from deep in her throat. "You don't really want me to tell you that now, do you? It would shatter the illusion... the fantasy."

"The mystery continues. I like that. You intrigue me, Miss Singleton."

"And you make me want to slap you." She wanted to fight the heat wave that was slowly taking over her body.

"Why? What did I do?" he said with a laugh.

"Someone has to slap that smugness out of you."

"Smug? I'm not smug," he argued.

"Please. I can't believe I'm the first to ever tell you that. You're smug, arrogant, haughty and domineering."

"Anything else?" he said with a smirk.

"You deliberately set out to make me feel small and inferior when I first entered your office. You wanted to play the role of the big, important professor who could control everything and everyone."

"You're getting me all wrong."

"You had me so flustered, I was like a babbling teenager ready to do anything to please you."

"And you didn't like that?"

"Of course. No self-respecting woman would. But coming from you, and knowing how you are or what people say about you...I didn't say I disliked it." Frowning, she cast her gaze to the floor.

He gently cupped her chin and brought her gaze back to his. "What is it then?"

Completely disarmed by his gentleness, Serena's breath caught in her throat a moment. Powerful men were always controlling and ruthless. They wanted what they wanted and didn't care... didn't care how she felt. Her feelings were always cast aside.

Looking into his eyes, she could clearly see he wanted her, but what did he want from her? What would he think if she spoke too much? "The truth is that I like it a little too much; more than what is healthy." There it was out. She'd said it. She held her breath.

Sebastian leaned in closer, his eyes smoldering. "Good," he whispered into her ear. "I think I can provide that for you, and you can provide what I need, too."

Chapter 6

The dinner hour was quickly approaching, but Serena longed to remain outside on the upper deck with Sebastian. They hadn't stopped talking since Michael had left them and she wanted to know more.

"I'll admit I've always found the idea of sending a child off to boarding school rather curious. Were you a naughty boy your mother couldn't handle?" Serena had gasped when Sebastian had spoken of his cold and isolated childhood.

He chuckled. "No. I was pretty much dark and moody, even back then. I was quiet and kept to myself. Music started to invade my life pretty young and all I ever wanted to do was play piano. No, boarding school was par the course. Everyone I knew went to boarding school."

"Did you miss your family while you were away?"

"At first, a bit, but I quickly made friends, and of course, music took an increasingly large part of my life. Soon music was all that mattered and a handful of

79

really good friends had become more important to me than the family I'd left behind."

He fell silent and Serena sensed he'd said too much.

"I think it's a little normal that you make strong bonds with friends. There's nothing to feel guilty or ashamed about."

"A little psych 101?" His grin was friendly, even affectionate, but his eyes put a definite end to the subject.

"I heard that you've been working on the score for a dark comedy."

"Actually, it's more like a dark romance. The trappings of love and all that."

"Something you know about?"

"Enough to be able to tap into it."

"Excuse me," a short, round bald man said as he approached them. "Mr. Sorensen, if you don't mind I'd like to introduce you to my wife and daughter. They're great fans and would appreciate a moment with you."

"Of course, Mr. Bresmin." Sebastian gave Serena's hand an apologetic squeeze. "I'll be back in just a minute."

"Take your time." Serena smiled as he walked away to greet his fans.

Much to the glee of the young teenager and a heavy set woman, he shook their hands and kissed their cheeks. It was the third time in twenty minutes that someone had come to him with such a request. He'd even received an invitation to make an appearance at a flamboyant woman's banquet the following week, something he'd regrettably declined.

Serena watched him. He carried himself with an air that was at once confident and charming. She considered the accusation she'd made earlier; calling him arrogant and smug. Watching him now she saw a whole different side of him. Even at a distance she could sense how approachable and warm he could be, given the right audience. As cold and distant as he'd seemed with Willow and her mother, he was now positively engaging and attentive to this young girl.

The realization suddenly struck her. Sebastian hadn't simply been invited because he was the son of the organizer of this fundraiser; he was here to draw in more people. *He* was the attraction. Of course. How had she not noticed it before? His name was important in Hollywood. His music had won several awards, including two Oscars and a Tony. Then again, his notoriety at the university was nothing to sneeze at.

He had everything, she concluded; looks, talent, smarts, money and looks. Oh, she thought with a private smile. She'd already said looks. Well, it was worth repeating.

After a few moments, Sebastian returned, a sincere grin that begged her forgiveness on his lips. "I'd promised myself I wouldn't leave your side again tonight, but I already find myself having to break that promise."

"I really hadn't suspected you'd be this popular."

"Yeah," he said with a wry chuckle. "A lot of people have underestimated me like that over the years."

Serena was about to defend her statement when she caught his teasing gaze.

"I'd forgotten all about it, but I have a little speech I have to give before dinner." He took her by the hand. "Come on. Everyone will be racing to the dining hall any minute now. I want to beat the rush."

Several people were already seated in anticipation of the dinner to come, but the vast majority of the large round tables were still empty. Pretty and elegantly draped in white, each table had an all white floral arrangement, white linen napkins and white china. The effect could have been stark and bare, but a touch of gold trim on the silverware and stemware as well as the sprinkling of green foliage among the pale blossoms gave depth and life to each table. The pure white also had a sobering effect. It brought home the charity they were all there for. Serena was impressed. Sebastian's mother really did know what she was doing.

"We'll be seated with my mother. I hope you don't mind." He pulled a chair out for her.

"I'm here to do as you wish. I don't think sitting through dinner with your mother will be all that bad." She looked down toward one end of the room then the other. A couple sat quietly at one table while a foursome of elderly gentlemen sat at another.

Serena sat down and noted that people were already streaming in behind them. Sebastian barely had time to sit down for two minutes before he was called to make his speech.

"Wish me luck," he said with a wink. "This crowd can be ruthless."

A buzz of quiet conversation filled the room. The scent of expensive perfume mingled with the gentle fragrance of the flowers on the table. When Sebastian took the microphone, all eyes turned to him. There was no need for him to ask for their attention; he already had it.

"I'm honored to stand before you tonight," he said, his voice strong and commanding. "Many of my family's closest friends are here and I can't begin to express my gratitude. My mother, Marika Sorensen, has a long standing relationship with the Children's Hospital and the money raised tonight will help rejuvenate a wing of the hospital, as well as buy much needed and very expensive medical equipment.

"As a childless man, many people assume I have no idea what it is like to have a sick child. True, I can't claim to have ever seen my own child suffer from the treatments for cancer or from the effects of any one of the many chronic children's diseases."

He looked down at the floor a moment and Serena could have sworn she'd heard him choke on the last few words. When he brought his gaze back to the crowd, his eyes were red and filled with emotion.

Her own eyes lined with tears. Serena couldn't imagine a man as haughty as he sometimes showed himself to be, could be so touching; so moving. With a hand that seemed to shake with emotion, he pulled a piece of paper out of his jacket pocket. The remainder of his speech, Serena assumed. But when he turned the paper to the audience, Serena realized it wasn't his speech at all.

"This is Paloma Lorre." Holding up the picture of a delightful little dark haired girl, he scanned the audience to ensure everyone got a good look. "When she was eight years old, she started to complain about a strange numbing sensation in her legs. Not long after her legs refused to function and she was unable to walk, unable to even stand. She was brought to the Children's and soon after that every part of her body began to shut down. Paralysis took over her entire body. The only thing Paloma could move were her eyeballs. The prognosis; Guillaume Barre Syndrome.

"For two and half long months, Paloma found herself in isolation. Her condition had become so critical, only her parents were permitted to see her. Doctors feared she'd never walk again." He let the

85

silence linger a long moment as everyone took in the disturbing information.

"I wonder if any of you here tonight can imagine; over a year shut up in a hospital. Your body has shut down and you can't remember the last time you had a breath of fresh air, the last time you played a game, the last time you had fun with friends.

"Paloma never let that get her down. Her determination and will got her through treatments and physiotherapy. Believe it or not, when Paloma finally left the hospital, it was on her own two feet. That is the power of research. That is the power of our money. That is the good that comes out of the small effort we ask of you tonight.

"The smile you see here, it's not just for the camera. It's always there. To hear this child talk and laugh, you'd never believe she'd ever suffered such pain. Yet, despite all the hardships she had to endure in her short life, she faced her days in the hospital with an optimistic view that is confounding.

"I know for a fact that most, if not all of you would whine, cry, complain and scream out your discontent if you'd ever had to endure even a fraction of what she's been through. You could perhaps say that she's not yet learned to be cynical, to be jaded, to be defeatist, to be pessimistic. I say she has the joy and determination to live, regardless what obstacles are thrown her way.

"For Paloma and all the other little valiant boys and girls who have had such obstacles put in their path, I ask you, men and women who've been graced with a charmed life, an easy life, to open your checkbooks and to be generous as you fill it in. As I look out at all of you, I know that many of you have built your own fortunes with your own blood, sweat and determination.

"Mr. Goldwater who successfully and solely built a real estate empire. Mr. and Mrs. Bingham who started their own line of high end children's clothes and are now in every elegant shop in America. Ms. Portman who borrowed a thousand dollars from a friend and turned it into a multi-million dollar beauty conglomerate.

"But I also know that many of you, Peter Bottom, Belinda Kyle, Garrett Thomas and Richard Lynch, to name but a few, have had your fortunes passed onto you by your hardworking parents. You've lived the coddled lives of silver spoon fed children.

You've never known hardship and barely know the meaning of the word struggle. If ever there was a time for you to step out and speak up for something worthwhile, to make a difference in the world, this is it.

"Our goal tonight is to raise twenty-five million dollars, a number I know is easily attainable. And rest assured; every last penny of it will go towards buying much needed equipment and repairing that broken down wing the hospital, no, the children so desperately need."

He put the picture away and stepped down. After a long, almost guilt-ridden silence, the elite crowd softly applauded him.

As he came towards her, Serena became vaguely aware of the people who'd joined her table. While she assumed they were Sebastian's family, she had no desire to make eye contact with them. Instead she looked at Sebastian as he came to the table and pulled out the chair besides her. She knew her open admiration was clear in her eyes, and she made no attempt to hide it. He was proving to be a surprise at every turn and she had to admit she enjoyed that.

"You don't mince words, do you?" she quietly said as he sat down.

Seated on the other side of him, his mother's glare was cold and hostile. Apparently she didn't share Serena's assessment of his speech, but she said nothing.

"This crowd needs to be shaken up sometimes. They get too comfortable, too complacent. They forget... or in many cases have never known what it's like to struggle, to hurt."

"I'm sure your speech will have the desired effect and you'll raise even more money than you've asked for."

He took the glass of white wine set before him and held it up to her. "Here's hoping."

"Your story about this little Paloma girl was very touching. How do you know her?" She bit down on the internal gnawing sensation that suggested he'd made it all up.

"She's the daughter of a colleague. He'd talked about her so much that he finally brought her into work to introduce her to us. She came to visit a few times after that; a beautiful little girl who instantly stole my heart, I must say."

Serena noticed an older, straight-back white haired man sitting beside Marika. He looked intently at Sebastian, a wistful smile barely warming the crease at his brow. He, too, seemed to disapprove of Sebastian's actions.

"Is that your father?" she asked, though she felt certain it was. They'd not been introduced and she couldn't help but wonder if it was intentional or just a slip.

Sebastian grinned and took a hold of her hand. He looked past his mother. "Father, I've neglected to introduce you to my date. Serena Singleton, this is Kaiser Sorensen."

Nodding, Serena smiled when she saw his warm, soulful eyes and sincere grin. "It's a pleasure to meet you."

While his eyes remained warm, he said nothing and Serena sensed Marika was the reason. Her back was glued to the chair as she stared straight ahead, her lips pursed in disapproval. After the brief introduction, she glared at her husband and clucked her tongue.

Kaiser was considerably older than Marika. That much was clear. And while he was a handsome man in his own right, Serena got the impression his love for Marika was based solely on her looks, on the impression she made on those around her. She was a beautiful woman and she surely went to great lengths to maintain that beauty. She was a trophy, but a slowly tarnishing one; one that constantly needed to be shined; one that constantly needed attention. Her resentment of that fact darkened her pretty pale eyes and probably would have creased her brow, had they had the liberty to do so.

Sebastian went on to introduce her to the other guests at the table. Willow was decidedly reserved when Sebastian introduced her as his date.

"Charmed," Mrs. Brookes said at the introduction, though her facial expression was anything but charmed. Clearly, she echoed her daughter's sentiment.

Seated immediately to Serena's left was Michael who leaned his knee into hers while Mr. and Mrs. Faris, introduced as close and dear friends of the family, rounded out the rest of the table.

Dinner was served amidst financial conversation that Serena found tedious and old. Michael did try to strike up a conversation that veered away from finances, but it always come back to the table. It seemed every topic came back to money. It sometimes began with art, but turned to the value of a Picasso. It sometimes began with a family vacation, but ultimately turned into an evaluation of this hotel, that cruise line or that exclusive boutique.

No matter how or where the conversation began, someone found a way to bring it back to money. How to make more. How to spend more. How to have more. Some didn't even bother disguising the discussion beneath anything else. They just came straight out and talked dollars and cents. While some lightly discussed wasting hundreds of thousands on some convoluted venture, others took to heart the thousands of dollars they'd put down on their dress, or their car, or their home.

"Are you enjoying your meal?" Sebastian said when he was finally able to tear away from his mother and pay some attention to Serena. He draped his arm on the back of her chair and leaned in close.

"Absolutely." She'd tried to ignore the sprinkling of words she'd picked up between him and his mother, but some of the words she'd overheard hurt her more than she cared to admit. Far from talking about money, Marika seemed obsessed with

Sebastian's future, namely his future with her. On more than one occasion she was referred to as, 'that girl,' and she thought she'd heard the term 'commoner' used to describe her.

Soothing those hurt feelings, however, was Sebastian's touch. The heat of his fingers as they drew a line across her bare shoulder was nothing compared to the heat of his gaze. For a brief instance, the room around them disappeared and she was alone with him. The heat became suffocating as his gaze intensified.

A waiter came around them and offered more wine, breaking the private and all too brief interlude.

"My mother insists on having the best chefs in her kitchen," he said after clearing his throat.

"It's understandable. With the crowd here, you don't want to just serve them something average and mundane."

"Taking my mother's defense. How admirable." He grinned.

"Is it just me, or do I sense a bit of tension between you and your mother?"

"If you look closely, you'll probably see there's a lot of tension between my mother and just about everyone in this room."

"That's a little harsh."

"That's the truth. As loving and kind as she can sometimes be, the demands of the role she has chosen to play among the obscenely rich sometimes takes its toll. I think much of it has whittled away the warm, compassionate woman she once was and has left a cold and calculating one in its place."

"Ouch," was all Serena could say. Saddened by his assessment of his own mother, she looked at him and wondered how he'd managed to come out unscathed by it all.

"Are you close to your parents?" he asked.

The workings of her fork on her plate suddenly took all her attention. She pushed the food around her plate a moment and swallowed the ball of emotion. She was more than willing to talk about him and his family, but was reluctant to open up about her own life.

"I'm sorry," he said in a voice that was soft and comforting. "Have I touched a chord?"

"My father left when I was eight." Her eyes remained on her plate as she made her declaration. "Other than his raging fits of anger and the back of his hand I don't remember much about him. My mother

94

tried to raise me alone, but her bottle was more important than I was. Before I turned nine, she drove herself off a pier."

Sebastian's warm hand enveloped her shoulder and pulled her closer. He said nothing, but she could feel his compassion for the childhood she'd had.

"It wasn't all that bad," she said after a long moment of relishing his comforting touch. "My Nana raised me; my mom's mother. She wasn't really prepared to take on a little, and rather hotheaded girl, but... well, she did what she had to do."

"Looking at you today, I'd say she did a pretty good job."

Pressing her lips tightly together as she remembered her grandmother, Serena looked at Sebastian. "That's far from what you said when I entered your office."

"I had my professional professor's hat on then. Now I'm your date. It's not the same thing."

"Bash," his mother's voice called over their quiet and private conversation. "Need I remind you there are other people at the table?"

He pulled away and sat back. "Yes, mother. Forgive me for being so attentive to my intriguing and fascinating date. I just can't pull away from her."

Marika sneered and shot him a killer glare. "Your father was just talking about the position he offered you at KSI."

"Was he?"

"It seems like it would be a wonderful opportunity for you. With Theodore Fiennes going into retirement, the timing couldn't be more perfect."

"From your vantage point, perhaps, Mother, not from mine. *Need I remind you* that I've students who depend on me, not to mention a musical score to finish?"

"Oh, honey. I haven't forgotten about this hobby of yours. What your father is offering, however, is a true career. He's offering not only financial stability, but the opportunity to become a financial force in your own right." Marika clucked her tongue and glanced briefly at Serena before leaning in to speak to Sebastian again. "You're standing in the community could be at risk if you insist on pursuing this musical nonsense much longer. The Brookes have been patient. I've been patient."

Her icy glare came to rest on Serena. "You can't spend the rest of your life surrounded by small minded musicians and…"

"That's enough, Mother. I won't have you insulting my date… my guest. I neither want nor need your advice; not about my career, not about my love life… not about my life in general."

Marika reached out to give his hand a patronizing tap. "Of course you don't dear. You've always been such a hothead."

"Don't worry about it, Bash," Willow called from across the table. "I think your hothead is your most endearing feature, but your mother is right."

"That's right, Bash," Mrs. Brooke threw in. "Music can only bring you so far in life. It's an amusing pastime, but hardly something you want to spend your life doing."

"And just think," Willow went on, "with you at KSI and me heading up my father's company, we'd be a true force to be reckoned with."

Michael leaned in close to Serena. "Really, I have to ask again. What is the draw of this man? I can understand the whole boy band ideology where tweens and teens are concerned. I can even understand the appeal of a real man like Elvis; I mean millions of women can't be wrong, right?"

Serena smiled and tried to be amused, but the frustration level was beyond manageable. The whole table had ganged up on Sebastian causing a fire to burn in her gut.

"I'll need your answer before next Friday, son," Kaiser said, his hands solemnly clasped before him. "I have to find a replacement for Theodore before he actually leaves us. You'd get that great corner office."

Sebastian cocked a cynical brow at his father. "Corner office? You think that'll do it for me? A corner office?"

"Bash, honey," Marika said. "Mind your manners. Your father is only trying to do what's best for you. Why can't you see that?"

Grinding his teeth, Sebastian dropped his gaze to his plate.

"I'm sorry." Mortified, Serena could not stay silent a moment longer. "Have any of you ever heard Sebastian's music? Have any of you ever bothered to sit back and truly listen to the melodies, the harmonies, the lyrical musicality of every single note he writes?"

For a long and uncomfortable moment, everyone at the table was silent. Though Michael seemed genuinely embarrassed for Sebastian, and Mr. and Mrs. Faris fidgeted in discomfort, everyone else seemed ready to pounce on Serena.

"You're his date for the night, darling," Marika snarled. "That hardly gives you the right to speak about the direction he should take in his life. I'm his mother. I raised him and I have a lifetime invested in him. I will not sit idly by and watch my son throw away his life, whether it be on a professional level or a personal one."

"Are you aware, Mrs. Sorensen, that your son has *thrown away* his life on a Tony and a few Oscars? Are you aware just how the world of music loves him, reveres him, admires him? He is not just a flash in the pan. He's the real deal. Every student at Irvine loves him, and while it might be easy to assume that it's just because he's sexy and good looking, I assure you they love him for what he brings to his music and what he can bring to their music."

"The man is well into his twenties and he still hasn't settled down," Marika argued with an indignant cluck of her tongue. "Does he really think a woman like Willow will just sit around and wait endlessly for him?"

Serena put her hand out and counted off on her fingers: "*The Flight. Sands of Time. Insane Love.* I bet you don't even know what all that is. Those are songs his students can only dream of writing. They're musical masterpieces that will far outlive everyone here."

Sebastian reached out to quiet her down with the gentle touch of his hand, but she was too impassioned to stop. "I cannot believe that you would try to silence such a musical genius."

"Serena, dear," Kaiser quietly said. "I appreciate your desire to defend Sebastian, but you are out of line. As Marika has stated, we have a lifetime invested in Bash. You have what? An invitation to a fundraiser?"

"No. Apparently I've been invited to a session of intimidation. How hypocritical of you. It's clear the only reason you invited Sebastian here is so that he could draw in loads of rich people. You want to profit from his celebrity all the while criticizing the very talent that made him so. You people disgust me." She threw her pretty linen napkin into her plate and stood.

100

"I think I've seen quite enough for one night. If you'll excuse me, I think I need to return to the world of the sane."

Six incredulous set of eyes stared back at her, but it was the amused smirk on Michael's face that caught her attention. She suddenly questioned her actions and wondered if she'd gone too far.

Somber faced and silent, Sebastian stood, took hold of her elbow and led her away.

Chapter 7

They walked to Sebastian's Roadster in silence. When Sebastian opened the passenger door for her, he barely looked at her. She sat and stared straight ahead as he got in and started the car. As he backed out of the parking space and headed to the street, she noticed the tight hold he had on the steering wheel as well as the hard and harsh manner in which he maneuvered the car.

"I'm sorry," Serena said after another few minutes of excruciating silence. Staring down at the pretty shoes Laura had loaned her, she cursed her hot temper. She'd put so much effort into looking as elegant and classy as she could, only to let her mouth show just how little class she actually had. "I'm so sorry I caused a scene, Sebastian... um, Professor Sorensen. I know this isn't..."

He continued to stare straight ahead as if she weren't there at all. Tears stung her eyes as she realized the fool she'd made of herself. She'd ruined everything. There was no way he'd consider being her advisor now. How stupid could she be?

Sebastian pulled the Roaster into a parking lot that overlooked the ocean. At any other times, this could have been romantic and dramatic. Now the ocean appeared dull and gray; unappealing in every way. When he killed the engine, Serena bit her lip in anticipation. Surely he would let her have it. Surely he would give her hell for meddling where she had no business meddling.

"No one has ever stood up for me like that before," he said in a quiet, almost crumbling voice.

"I know it was none of my business…"

He reached for her hand and brought it to his lips. "I've long passed the day when I need someone to speak for me, but… I have to admit, I enjoyed that. You came to my defense in a way I never could."

While she remained calm and serene on the outside, inside she trembled from the electric shock that shot through her. His touch was like fire, burning through her skin while his words reached deep down inside her.

"So you're not mad?" she managed to say.

"Far from it. If anything I'm even more fascinated by you than I already was." He sat back and leaned into the headrest. Closing his eyes he let out a long and exasperated breath. "My family," he grunted. "They take some getting used to."

His last words were slightly slurred and his fingers slipped slowly away from hers and went to his belly. She wondered if he'd not had too much to drink. Wine had flowed freely at the fundraiser, but she had only seen him take two or three glasses throughout dinner. Had he taken more and she simply hadn't noticed?

"You know, you've had a big night," Serena said. "Why don't you let me do the driving?"

Without opening his eyes, he said, "No, I'm fine. I'll get you home."

"Why? Don't you trust me to drive this thing?" She added a teasing tone to her voice hoping to avoid a drunken argument.

Still leaning into the headrest, he turned to look lazily at her, a crooked smile on his lips. "You want to try driving it?"

"Sure. Could be fun." Without waiting for him to change his mind, she got out of the car and ran around to open his door.

Though he struggled to get to shaky feet, he tried to laugh it off. Walking the palms of his hands along the side of his car to keep his balance, he made his way to the passenger seat and got in.

"Aren't you going to buckle up?" Serena said as she got in and started the car, but he was already out. She reached passed his limp body and pulled the seatbelt across him. "Let's get you home, music man."

She eased the car onto the road and though she lacked his skill with the smooth curves, she managed to make it to her place in one piece. The moment she pulled into the parking space beside her own car, she realized she'd not really solved the problem; she'd only brought it home.

Now that they were at her place, what was she going to do with him?

"Sebastian, can you hear me?"

"Baby, baby, baby. I hear you loud and clear. Are you having trouble with my Roadster?"

Amused by his uncharacteristic silly antics, Serena helped get him out of the car.

"You know," he said as she guided him up the stairs, "I don't think I really feel so good."

"No." She shook her head as they reached her floor and she propped him up against the wall beside her door. "You really don't."

Once she'd unlocked the door, she kicked it open and led Sebastian inside. The moment he stepped inside, he vomited all over her freshly cleaned hardwood floor.

"Okay," she said with surprising calm. "You really don't feel good." Gripping his shoulders, she led him to the sofa and let him fall back. "I'll go clean up your little mess and be right back."

"Wow, I can't remember the last time I've felt so…" He gagged, but quickly brought it under control.

Serena quickly picked up his mess, but between his gagging and the awful smell of partially digested meal, she found herself rushing to the bathroom to throw cool water on her face.

"You okay?" Sebastian called out.

"Yeah."

Before he could be sick again, she hurried to the cabinet under the kitchen sink and pulled out a bucket. "Here," she said as she came up and shoved it beside him. "Use this if you still feel nauseated."

He sat up as he chocked and gagged and retched, but nothing came out and he reclined once again. "Get me out of this," he muttered as he tugged on his tie.

As she pulled the knot of his tie apart and unbuttoned the first button of his shirt, she noticed how hot his skin was. It wasn't the smoldering and sexy heat she'd felt early, but an unhealthy hotness that left his skin ashy and clammy.

Suddenly sensing the urgency of his situation, she worked to free him of his jacket, shirt and pants and quickly snuggled him up in a large and soft fleece gray sweatshirt and university sports shorts.

"Come on," she said as she tried to sit him up. "Let's get you into bed."

He swayed and sank back into the cushions.

"Sebastian, I can't get you to your feet if you don't help me."

When she tried again, he groaned and she knew this was more than just a little too much to drink.

"Okay, let's forget getting you into bed. We've got to get you to the hospital."

Chapter 8

"I initially thought he'd had too much to drink," Serena said to the triage nurse. "It's only when I noticed how feverish he'd become that I realized something was wrong."

When the nurse frowned and didn't say anything, Serena felt uneasy. She glanced at the woman's name tag. "Um, Nurse Miller, do you think it could perhaps be something serious."

Nurse Miller nodded as she efficiently pulled up the sweatshirt and gently prodded Sebastian's hard abdomen. Serena watched her, mesmerized by the movements of the woman's fingers over his skin, efficient, but almost sensual. Even as sick as he was, Sebastian managed to have that effect on women. From the admiring look in Nurse Miller's eyes, no doubt she was attracted to Sebastian. Serena couldn't help but feel a tug of envy.

Sebastian was pale, but he fought to remain upright. His knuckles were white as they gripped the edge of the examination table.

"Do you know what he ate?" the nurse asked.

"Hmm, we had an appetizer with escargots in a creamy sauce. After that he had…" Serena gazed at Sebastian. She hadn't really paid much attention to what had been on his plate.

"Duck," he grunted.

"How many drinks?" Though the question was aimed at Sebastian, Nurse Miller looked pointedly at Serena.

"A glass of champagne before dinner and a few glasses of wine with his meal. I didn't see him take anything else." Serena was tempted to tell the young nurse who Sebastian Sorensen was exactly. Not that she wanted him to have special treatment, but… perhaps she'd move him along a little faster if she knew who he was. She gazed at Sebastian and wondered why he didn't mention it himself. Why didn't he demand the VIP treatment affluent people always seem to believe they deserved?

"No after dinner liquor?" the nurse went on. "No cognac, no brandy or anything like that?"

"No, we left right after the main course."

She cocked a brow. "Okay. Looks like it could be a little bit of food poisoning, but we'll get him tested to see what's really going on. How are you feeling?"

"Me? Fine. Perfect."

"Do you know if anyone else fell ill at the dinner?"

"No. Like I said, we left right after dinner."

"Okay, well, let us know if you start to feel any signs of queasiness or fever."

Serena nodded.

Another nurse entered and her eyes immediately popped wide open when she looked at Sebastian. Her tight and stressed lips turned into a bright smile and she beckoned her colleague to the far end of the small room. They whispered a private exchange for a few moments, both glancing repeatedly at Sebastian.

When Nurse Miller finally returned to them, her demeanor had considerably softened. "I'm sorry, Mr. Sorensen. It seems I didn't recognize who you are."

Sebastian let out a dry chuckle and coughed then gagged and threw up, making a mess of the white tiled floor. The newly arrived nurse hurried out to find someone to get the mess cleaned up.

"Does that mean you'll get him tested faster?" Serena asked.

The nurse shot a professional glare at Serena. "No. He'll get tested quickly because he shows serious symptoms, not because of his celebrity status. What his status will allow, however, in addition to the expansive health insurance he has, is a private room the moment he's been tested."

Pleased to see he'd get the prompt care he needed, Serena smiled and let the nurse finish her examination of her patient.

"I'll have someone bring you to an examination room right away. In the meantime, I'll make sure your room is prepared and ready."

The nurse left them and went into the small office adjacent to the triage room.

Sebastian looked at Serena. "It's late and you must be exhausted. You don't have to stay, Serena. You've already done enough."

"I can't just leave you here. I'll stay until you're settled in your room and then we'll see." When he remained silent, she added, "Unless you want me to leave."

"Not at all. I want you here, but I would never dream of imposing."

The nurse returned just as an intern arrived with a wheelchair.

After being wheeled away, he was tested and all that remained to do was wait for the results in his room.

Serena was surprised by the serene décor of the hospital room that resembled that of an elegant, and quaint country inn. The colors on the wall were warm and inviting. The comforter on the bed was thick and homey. They'd even put a beautiful vase of flowers on the large dresser in front of the window.

"If they spoil me too much, I won't want to go home," Sebastian said as the intern helped him into bed.

The young man smiled. "We want you to be comfortable, Mr. Sorensen. You're welcome to stay as long as you like, but, to be honest, I think you'll be tired of being up here soon enough." He tucked Sebastian in, nodded a salutation at Serena and left.

"How you feeling?" Serena said as she came to rest her fingers on his forehead. "You're still burning up."

"I'm strong. I can take it." He offered her a sly, but weak grin.

"Yeah, well, I think it's the clean up crew who can't take it anymore. You left a pretty distinctive trail from triage to here."

He shook his head. "Every time I think – okay, that's it, I have nothing more in my gut – I'm wrong. When I least expect it... there it comes again."

The last few bouts of vomiting had been virtually dry vomits. He gagged and gagged, but there in fact was nothing left to expel. His voice showed the strains. It'd become more raw and hoarse with every bout.

"My mouth feels dry and disgusting."

"I'll go get you a glass of water." In the little bathroom of his room, she ran the cold water and called out. "I think I have a few breath mints in my purse."

"I'm not a fan of breath mints, but tonight I'll make an exception." He took the glass of water and took a swallow then accepted the breath mint.

"Better?" she said.

He nodded. "Thanks. You're too good to me. I could get used to this." Pushing his head deep into the thick pillow, he suddenly reached for her hand and held on tight.

Though he didn't groan or grumble or complain, Serena could see by the beads of sweat on his brow, by the speed with which the color left his face and by his tightly closed eyes that his gut was acting up again.

"Is there anything I can do to make you more comfortable?" Serena said.

His fingers tightened around hers just as a tight grimace came to his face.

She pulled a chair up beside the bed and sat down. "Maybe I should call your parents."

"Why bother?" he grunted. "Do you really think they'll drop everything and come running to see their ill son?"

Serena chocked. How could he say such a thing? She knew he'd been sent to boarding school and he'd mentioned of the strained relationship he'd always had with his parents, but this? He was sick. He was in the hospital. How could they ignore that?

"Aren't you exaggerating, Sebastian?"

He shrugged. "Go ahead. Call them. You'll see." He grimaced and groaned as he squeezed her hand to the point of pain.

"There must be something I can do." She felt so helpless just watching him suffer.

"I'm okay."

"I have an idea," she whispered. Still holding onto his hand, she reached for her purse and pulled out her ipod. "Here." She set the ipod on the mattress beside his shoulder and put one earpiece in his ear then leaned in close as she put the other earpiece in her own ear. She quickly found the song she wanted to play.

As *The Flight* played into their ears, his fingers relaxed around hers. The soothing strings, the plaintive brass and the haunting woods brought them on a journey of heartache, joy, pain and love. As Serena's emotions rode on the melody, she felt certain Sebastian was right there with her, traveling on every chord.

The crease of his brow was gone as was the tightness in his jaw.

"Your music is beyond magical, Sebastian. It heals." She set her head on the pillow beside his. "I can't tell you the number of times I've listened to these songs."

Serena heard the soft shuffle of rubber soles on the tiled floor and reluctantly opened her eyes as she turned down the volume of her ipod. A young nurse stood in the doorway admiring the scene.

"I'm so sorry to disturb you," she said. "I just wanted to let Mr. Sorensen know that we tried to contact his family, but…" She shifted her weight and seemed uncomfortable.

Sebastian released Serena's hand and grunted. "See what I told you? What did my fine, upstanding parents have to say?"

"Hmm, we spoke to your mother and she said she'd try to pass by after…" She coughed and shot an embarrassed gaze at Serena.

"The fundraiser. Yeah, yeah. How could my mother possibly leave the posh yacht filled with important people to tend to her sick little boy?" Sliding his index finger across his thumb, indicating money, he let out an annoyed sigh.

"Anyway," the nurse went on. "Someone should pass by tomorrow morning to see you."

"Don't look so brokenhearted, sweetie. It's not like I'm dying or something." He shot a cynical gaze toward Serena. "Not that that would change much."

116

The nurse looked at Serena. "I was told you may have eaten the same things as Mr. Sorensen. You still have no symptoms?

"No. I'm fine."

"Okay then. I'll go see if the test results have come in yet."

Sebastian leaned back.

"I know it's little consolation, but I'm here, Seb," Serena said.

A slow, lazy smile came to his lips, but his eyes remained closed. "That's a big consolation." He reached for her fingers. "Do you have *Insane Love* on there?"

"Of course." Pleased she'd not left her ipod at home, but had kept it in her purse, she started the song and resumed her position on the pillow beside him.

Before the song was over, she heard a soft and gentle snore come from Sebastian. Moments later she, too, drifted off and was awakened when Sebastian squeezed her hand and suddenly sat upright.

"Are you okay?"

His breath came in short sharp gasps and Serena reached for the emergency button beside his bed.

"Don't," he grunted.

"What's wrong? What's going on?"

"It was just a nightmare. It's nothing." He sank back into the pillows and closed his eyes, but his grip on her fingers remained tight, almost desperate.

"The doctor should come around with the results soon. I'll see if he can't give you anything to help you sleep."

"I'm okay," he muttered as he drifted off again.

Studying his face, she saw how the pain, whether from his belly ache or from another disturbing nightmare, played on lips as they tugged down, mouthed silent words and parted in fear. The crease of his brow fluctuated, accompanying the constantly changing play of his lips.

"Mrs. Sorensen," the soft spoken doctor said as he entered the room. Tall and lanky, he looked down at Serena then at Sebastian's prone figure.

Serena popped out the earpiece and stood. "I'm Miss Singleton, a friend of Sebastian's." Taking an eager step toward the doctor, she hoped he'd finally have the results.

"I'm Doctor Nguyen. You must be a pretty good friend to still be here in the middle of the night."

118

"Yes, well, we can't reach his parents, so… I can't just leave him here alone. He's been having nightmares and is very agitated."

"Does he often have nightmares?"

"I don't know. I don't know him that well." The last word came out as a regretted grunt.

"The agitation and fitful sleep could be a result of the nausea and fever."

"Have the results come in yet? Do you know why he's so sick all of a sudden?"

"Nothing definitive. These things can be tricky sometimes. We've tested for the usual suspects and they all came back negative. Now we have to look at more… shall we say, suspicious culprits."

"What do you mean?"

"We've ruled out food poisoning."

"What are you saying?"

"I'm not saying anything yet, Miss Singleton. Please don't jump to conclusions. I'm just telling you that we don't have a definitive answer yet."

Sebastian groaned.

"I'll pass by to check up on him a little later. Don't hesitate to let a nurse know if anything changes."

Serena hurried back to Sebastian's side as the doctor walked out.

"Stay with me." Sebastian said.

"The doctor was just here, Seb. They still don't have the results, but he'll be back the moment they do." As she reached him she realized, however, that his eyes were closed and he was talking in his sleep.

"No," he called out. "Don't leave me!"

"I'm here, Seb. I'm here." She had no idea who he was calling out to in his dream, but she wanted him to know that she was there; that someone was there with him… for him.

He grabbed her hand with fierce force and she let out a soft yelp of pain. With her free hand, she wiped his brow then gently ran her fingers through his hair. He immediately slackened his grasp.

"I'm here," she whispered. "I won't leave."

Tears clung to his lashes as he struggled through the dream that so tormented him. She felt helpless for a brief moment then decided to try to wake him. Leaning over him, she kissed his brow and softly whispered his name.

He stirred and groaned, but remained deep in sleep.

"Sebastian, you're having a nightmare. Wake up, and everything will be okay." Again she kissed his brow while her fingers continued to play through his hair.

"I want you with me," he muttered, the desperate and fearful voice of his nightmare now strangely husky, almost aroused. The fingers that had clasped around hers moved up to grab her forearm and pull her closer.

She sat on the edge of the bed before he could break her arm, and tried to make sense of what was happening. He was asleep and clearly had no idea what he was doing, but... She was awake. She knew she should back away, but her body... her body wanted the heat of his, wanted the touch of his fingers on her skin... wanted him.

He pulled her closer, murmuring incoherently as he did so. His breath warmed her face and the longing to kiss him became unbearable. For a long, torturous moment, her lips hovered over his. It would be so easy, so delicious... just one small kiss... just one taste of his...

As she battled with her lustful desires, Sebastian brought his free hand to the small of her

121

back and pressed her to him. A shockwave of heated intensity coursed through her, enveloped her and she felt powerless to stop her reaction. She leaned in closer, inhaling his breath. Her lips parted and she closed her eyes. He was all she wanted. In that moment, he was all that mattered. Without a doubt, she knew she could easily do anything he asked of her. Her body was willing and her mind was mush.

It'd been so long… too long… and his touch ignited a flame she'd intentionally doused with cold water for over a year.

Her lips brushed against his just as the sound of *Sands of Time* sounded in the earpiece that lay on the pillow beside Sebastian. She pulled away, initially startled by the powerful opening notes of the song that had so often stirred so many emotions.

Music. All her energy had been put into her music, her career, her love and passion. Was she going to throw it all away on a fling with Sebastian Sorensen? Despite the painful protest of her body, she pulled away and twisted her arm out of his grasp.

He murmured a complaint, but remained asleep and after a few more murmurings, he quieted down and slept peacefully.

Staring at him, she saw her past, her present and her future flash before her. She'd been through so much, had worked so hard and knew more work was still to come to get to this point in her life. "It kills me to pull away from your touch," she whispered. "But I have to think of what's best for me; not just the instant gratification, but what's best for my future."

She kissed her fingertips and touched her fingers to his lips. "You're dangerously sexy, Mr. Sorensen; too sexy for my own good."

Chapter 9

The room was chilly and dark when Sebastian opened his eyes. Scanning the room he tried to find familiar ground. The past hours were a blur of fever, headaches and punches in the stomach that pestered his sleep and left him gripping the sheets in sweat.

His last memory was of the fundraiser. Serena... she'd defended him, stood up for him. A man of lesser self worth could have easily been insulted by her outburst, but he'd been touched not only by the way she'd spoken to his parents, but the words she'd said about his work. Far from needing praise and compliments, he'd enjoyed every word she'd said. Something about the intensity of her words had held more weight than the critical acclaim he'd received.

Of course, there had also been that minor slip about how handsome and sexy he was. Or had that been intentional? He grinned at the thought then, like a shot, he sat upright and tried to remember what had happened to her. He didn't remember dropping her off, didn't remember going to her place. She'd been with him as they'd left the yacht and he clearly remembered her at his side when he'd pulled over to thank her for coming to his defense.

But then…

His eyes, aided by the dim light that peaked around the curtains, adjusted to the darkness and he was able to better make out his surroundings. None of it made sense until he realized Serena was right there beside him.

Seated awkwardly in the small armchair she'd pulled up to the bed, her head rested on a tiny corner of his pillow. Lost deep in sleep, her lips pouted with innocence and sweetness. She was as lovely sleeping as she was dripping in sensuality at the fundraiser. He'd never had a woman sleep with him overnight before. Never even wanted that much of a commitment. Now he can see how he wanted to see Serena sleeping like an angel like this more often. The tender thought unnerved yet thrilled him at the same time.

Slowly the events of the previous night came back to him; the sudden onset of nausea and the cramps, the fever. She'd been there through triage, through the tests… had she really been there throughout the night?

The music. Yes, he remembered. When the nightmares and pain kept him from sleeping, she'd found the way to calm him. Touched by her compassion, he brushed her hair off her face. "My own family didn't even bother coming," he whispered.

She stirred, and while he regretted waking her when clearly she couldn't have slept well throughout the night, he was nonetheless happy to see her big green eyes looking up into his.

"You're awake." Serena sat up and ran her fingers through her tousled hair.

"Had I known you'd be spending the night I would have made room for you up here," Sebastian said with a wicked grin while his palm patted the mattress beside him.

A rosy blush colored her cheeks as she offered him a reserved smile. "I don't think the nurses would approve. Already I had to argue with them every night for them to allow me to stay at all."

"Every night?" For the first time he noticed that she was no longer wearing the beautiful gown she'd worn to the fundraiser. In tight jeans that hugged her

126

tight rear end and a bright red loose knit sweater that outlined her perfect round breasts, she was even sexier and more beautiful than when he'd last seen her. Her hair was a mess and she wore little make up, but... he couldn't remember the last time a woman had affected him so profoundly.

He felt an unexpected tightening in his boxer briefs, thinking how good it would feel to have her naked against him.

"Yes," she said, her eyes showing the concern she felt for him. "You've been here for three nights."

"What?"

"They had to pump your stomach. They never found what caused you to be so violently sick. I spoke to your mother."

Sebastian sank back into the pillow and closed his eyes.

"I had to let her know how you were doing, but I also wanted to ask if anyone else had gotten sick that night."

"She must have been thrilled by that." His grunt was a little rougher than he'd intended.

"Well, I'll admit she seemed to think I was insinuating her chefs had screwed up, but I told her I

127

just wanted to make sure you'd gotten sick due to something else entirely."

Turning to look at her, he took her hand and guided her around so that she sat on the edge of the bed. "Thank you. She might not show it, but I'm sure she appreciated all you've done for me."

Her skin glowed and her eyes were alert despite the lack of sleep. Her gaze only vaguely veiled her admiration of him. He knew he pleased her; knew he appealed to her, yet she was decidedly restrained. It was both intriguing and alluring. For as long as he could remember women had thrown themselves at him. It'd been amusing for a while, but he'd quickly grown tired of the easy women. Boredom set in when all he had to do was look at a woman and she eagerly did his bidding.

Women's lib... yeah right. Not in his circle. The women that hovered around him were more than willing to rely on a man, or at least on his wallet, to make them happy. A throwback to the 1950s and happy to be dependent on a man, like his own mother. Social status and being able to keep that trust money within its own circle was what these women cared about, not so much marrying for love. Despite how he

128

avoided commitment like a plague, he was a romantic deep down. His music was an outlet of that romantic energy and sensitivity. It was the way he communicated it, while still being the man's man that he was, the alpha, who liked being in charge and taking what he wanted when he wanted. That is, until now. His sensitive vulnerable side was showing, spilling over since he first met this woman who was pushing every button of his. Serena Singleton, whose very presence evoked the strongest possessive emotions he'd ever felt for a woman. She was every inch as feminine and elegant as his mother's social circle of women, yet independent, tough, and strong-minded at the same time. She didn't need a man to make her feel whole or to please her, and that made her even more enticing. Serena held her own in every way and seemed determined to do so.

"Why did you stay?" he asked.

"I couldn't just leave you here alone. It just didn't seem right."

"Looks like I really got more than I bargained for when you walked into my office. You're far from the needy, desperate, inept girl I thought you were. I owe you one."

"Really? Thanks for your compliment, I think," Serena said.

"It is...I don't usually have patience for desperation or ineptness; but with you, let's just say I'm glad I took a chance on you."

"Again, thank you, I think," Serena let a half smile escape while closing her eyelid halfway.

He could see the excitement in her eyes and knew it had nothing to do with getting closer to him. It was at the prospect of having him as her advisor. His ego could have been dented by that fact, but it only added to her appeal. She wouldn't be easy. She'd be the challenge he'd come to long for, and he would greatly reward her for ultimately giving into him. He felt himself growing harder just anticipating it.

She wanted him as his advisor... she had no idea what awaited her. Such innocence... He would teach her things she'd never imagined. He would bring her to heights of ecstasy few mortals ever experienced. He would revel in the touch of her skin, the taste of her mouth, the secrets of her body. Already, he could imagine how delicious she would taste when he explored her entire body with his mouth and lips. He couldn't wait to make her moan out his name when he pounded into her and bring her to climax. It would be the greatest pleasure hearing sweet innocent Serena Singleton cry out in ecstasy.

"I was going to ask how you're feeling, but judging by that silly grin on your face, I'd say you're feeling pretty good right about now."

"Indeed," he said, crossing his legs.

Chapter 10

"Are you sure you're going to be able to drive yourself home?" Serena said as she reluctantly got out of Sebastian's car.

Touched by her concern for him he was tempted to take her up on her offer to drive him home. Aside from a few dizzy spells he felt fine, but he dreaded leaving her. "I think you've done enough. I'm already heavily indebted to you."

"Call me if you need anything." She shut the car door and turned away.

"I most certainly will." He sat watching the gentle sway of her hips as she walked to her apartment building. Her tight jeans left little to the imagination and he could already imagine how perfectly her buttocks would fill his hands. "I will surely need something and I will surely call you for it."

With a regrettable chuckle, he put the car into drive and headed home. With every turn his thoughts left Serena and turned to the events of the fundraiser. He wanted to believe it'd been a simple matter of food poisoning. The matter would be settled; over and done with. If it had been food poisoning, however, he wouldn't have been the only one to get sick. In addition, the doctor had all but conclusively eliminated the possibility. He didn't want to allow his mind to suspect other possibilities, but the thoughts gnawed at him. Who? Why?

Parking his car in the underground garage he went through the rolodex in his head, but found no one who would want him any harm. As he rode up in the elevator, he glanced at his reflection in the mirror and chuckled.

"Seems Cinderella has turned into a pumpkin," he muttered as he pulled on the old gray sweatshirt. When he got a good look at his sports shorts, he laughed out loud. "Nice, Serena."

The doors of the elevator slid open and he walked into his penthouse apartment. His mother's favorite vase, the one that adorned the side table of his main entrance, was in a million pieces on the floor. At first he wanted to consider the possibility of a strong wind. It wouldn't be the first time. Several months before he'd found papers strewn across the entire apartment when he'd neglected to close his bedroom window.

Another step brought him into the main living area and he instantly knew this wasn't a simple matter of an open window. Someone had ransacked his apartment. Every cushion of his posh sofa was torn apart. Treading carefully he walked to the kitchen and found every drawer pulled out and every cabinet door opened.

Even his refrigerator had been emptied.

He dreaded going into his bedroom. The door was ajar and he could already see a pile made up of his fine Italian suits. "Damn it," he muttered as he pushed the door open. As expected every drawer had been pulled out of the dresser and the contents thrown onto the bed. Not a hanger remained hanging in the closet.

Among the clothes, ties and boxers on the bed; he saw his favorite cuff links, the gold chain his mother had given him and the diamond lapel pin he'd won at a social function. Whoever had broken into his apartment had obviously not been looking to steal valuables.

Then what had they wanted? He couldn't imagine, but instantly thought of his parents. Were they safe? He headed back to the elevator and punched the button for the garage level. If he'd been targeted, perhaps his parents had been as well. He pulled out his cell phone and prepared to call them when it vibrated in his hand.

It was Serena. He realized on seeing her name on the screen just how badly he wanted to talk to her. "Serena."

"Sebastian, I'm sorry to bother you. I hope you weren't resting."

"Not quite. What's up?" He hoped he sounded casual.

"I forgot to tell you I have your tuxedo. I had it cleaned yesterday and picked it up this morning, but didn't think to bring it to the hospital."

"Serena, you didn't have to go to the trouble of having it cleaned."

"Yeah," she said with an amused snort. "I'm guessing you don't remember throwing up on it, do you?"

He laughed despite the stress he felt. The elevator door opened and he hurried to his car. "No, I don't remember that."

"Well, if you'd smelled what I smelled when I first came back to my place, you would have rushed to the dry cleaners too. Poor Mr. Lowry. You should have seen his face when I brought it in. I think if it'd been up to him he would have thrown it out rather than clean it."

"Hey, that's an Armani," Sebastian said with a grin. He slid into the driver's seat of his Roadster. Amazed at how soothing the sound of her voice was, he sat back and exhaled slowly.

"Do you want me to pass by later on a drop it off? Or maybe…"

At that moment he would have liked nothing more than to have her drop by. It was a little premature to say he already missed her, but he had to admit he looked forward to seeing her again. "Look, why don't you hang onto it? I'll come by to get it when I have a chance."

"Sure." There was a long moment of hesitation. "Sebastian? Are you okay?"

"Yeah, fine." Though he would have liked to share this new development in this disastrous week, he held back. This was all turning out to be a little too strange for his liking; the sudden poisoning that wasn't

136

as accidental as he'd originally thought and now this break in. What were the chances the two episodes were related? What were the chances the person who broke into his place knew he'd be out for the night?

"Okay then," Serena said in a soft, almost shy voice.

"I have a few things to take care of. You wouldn't believe what can pile up when you're in the hospital for a few days. I'll call you the first free minute I get."

"Oh, okay. I'll just leave it hanging in the hall closet then. Bye."

"Bye." He chuckled softly as he ended the call. He'd heard that shy hesitation before and it made her all the more enticing. His body ached as he thought of all he wanted to do to her. It ached for all she did to him. He'd long given up on ever finding a woman who had that special blend of naiveté and sophistication, innocence and mystery. Of course there was the student/professor problem he had to work out, but he felt confident he could work his way around it. The scenarios that played in his mind, pushing her up against the bookshelf while she wore a skirt with nothing underneath, taking her on top of his desk,

137

hiding her under his desk while she took him into her mouth during a serious meeting with a school official or someone stuffy or uptight like that. "Yes, I'm going to enjoy weaving my way into your life, Serena." And certainly into your pants.

He started the car and headed to his parents.

Chapter 11

Traffic was annoying heavy as he tried to make his way to his father's office, but going there was quicker than driving out to his parents' home and he was certain he'd get a sense of what was happening just by seeing his father's face.

With growing impatience he tapped his fingers on the steering wheel. He'd barely advanced a few yards in the past fifteen minutes. Before he lost it and leaned into the horn he brought his thoughts back to Serena.

The only thing that kept him from calling her was the risk of needlessly alarming her. He felt agitated and knew it'd show in his voice. She'd already done so much for him and he didn't want to burden her with his problems more than necessary.

A break in traffic allowed him to advance just enough to squeeze off the highway and out into the city streets. Although traffic lights rendered the trip stop and go, he managed to arrive at his father's prestigious waterfront offices within ten minutes.

Newport Harbor; it was an impressive and beautiful place to work, Sebastian thought. At least as far as working in an office was concerned. Everything about the building was rich and ostentatious. The marble floors gleamed and the brass fixtures shined.

In the elevator he anticipated the type of welcome he'd receive once the doors slid open. Would his father be relieved to see him up and about? Would he question what had happened? Would he show the slightest sign of caring at all?

He was a grown man; a grown man who didn't understand why he still sought the love and acceptance of his parents. He hated himself for needing his father's approval so much, but couldn't rid himself of that need. He also hated how much he was still tied to them…he knew his obligations as a Sorensen, the only heir to the mass fortune and empire. It was the only reason why he was even friends with Willow, who seemed to understand and want to run the Sorensen empire.

The elevator doors parted and his heart raced. With quiet and reluctant footsteps, he approached the desk of his father's secretary.

"Hello, Miss Goldwater."

The young platinum blond woman looked up and immediately smiled. It was a warm smile that was accompanied by a now familiar look of lust in her eyes.

"Sebastian." She stood and leaned over her desk to give him a hug. Dressed in a prim grey pantsuit she was the height of professionalism, but the pantsuit couldn't hide her voluptuous curves. "What brings you up here? I thought you were working at the university."

"Yeah, I am." He couldn't help but notice the complete lack of concern for his recent ordeal. Obviously his father had not even bothered to mention to the people around him what had happened to his son. "I just stopped by to see my father. Is he in?"

Pressing her lips into a tight regrettable line, she looked at him. "He's with someone. One of his big hush hush meetings."

"Any idea how long he'll be?"

She shrugged. "They've been in there for over three hours already. Either they'll step out any minute now or they'll be in there for the rest of the day. Your guess is as good as mine."

"Okay." He looked around, glanced at his watch and returned his gaze to her. "Well, I'll take a chance and wait a bit. It's almost noon so hopefully they'll take a break for lunch."

"That's a fair bet."

Sebastian turned to the austere beige, black and chrome waiting room. Modern to the point of being uncomfortable, he'd always suspected his father had chosen such a modern, almost hip décor to compensate for his graying hair and aging body.

As he waited he pulled out his cell phone and called his agent. After listening to the phone ring a half dozen times he hung up and tried Rick Steinberg, the film producer.

"Mr. Steinberg's office," a soft professional voice said.

"Mr. Steinberg, please."

"Who may I say is calling?"

"Sebastian Sorensen."

"Just one moment, Mr. Sorensen."

A robotic message about the merits of the production house's latest movie had time to play three times over before Rick answered.

"Sebastian! How's my music man feeling?"

"Hi, Rick. That's exactly what I wanted to call you about. It appears I skipped an important meeting with you. I know you were looking forward to hearing how the score to your movie was coming along. I'm terribly sorry, but I…"

"Hey, don't worry about it. I heard you were feeling a little under the weather lately."

"What do you mean? How'd you hear about it?"

"When you didn't show, I tried to call you. I didn't get an answer so I tried a few hours later; still no answer. The following day I tried a dozen times and an angelic voice finally answered. She quickly explained that she'd found your cell phone was in your jacket pocket… the jacket you apparently left at her place. I guess you had a bit of fun before you got sick." He chuckled.

"To tell you the truth, I couldn't tell you. I was out before I could even have that bit of fun."

"Too bad. Anyway, she seemed like a lovely young woman who appears to care somewhat for your sorry ass. She let me know you were in the hospital."

"So Serena told you." Sebastian said with a warm smile.

"Sorry. Didn't catch her name. Serena, is it? A beautiful name for a beautiful voice. She just said you would be unreachable for a few days. Something about food poisoning."

"I guess I owe her one."

"I don't know. I'd say you owe her more than just one." Rick laughed.

"Right."

"Look, take it easy and give me a call when you want to reschedule. I'm still looking forward to hearing this work of genius you've been working on."

"Sure thing." Sebastian ended the call just as the door to his father's office opened.

"Sebastian!" Kaiser said when he saw him. "What are you doing up here?"

Sebastian approached him but stopped short when he saw a tall and handsome blonde young man about thirty-two years old in a grey custom-tailored suit and white linen shirt step out. With clean cut blond hair and piercing blue eyes, he looked like an European male model. The planes of his face were sharp and angular, but his lips were curled up in a victorious grin. Something about him seemed familiar, and he couldn't quite put his finger on it. For a long moment the two men looked at each other, sizing each other up.

One dark and brooding, the other fair and calculating. Both young, tall and fit. The way the blonde man was staring at him in a challenging manner, had his defenses up.

"I had a few things I wanted to ask you," Sebastian said with an uncharacteristic hesitation, "but... I could come back later."

"No. No. It's just as well you stopped by when you did. Son, I'd like you to meet Price Turnsby."

"Yes, you looked familiar." Sebastian accepted the finely manicured hand Price put out, and returned the strong handshake.

Price nodded. "Ah, yes, probably the society pages. I hope you don't believe everything you read. Those stories about me and that young woman were greatly exaggerated."

"I wouldn't really know about that. I was talking more about a photo I saw in Times magazine. You were among the top ten young billionaires."

"Ah, yes, that. If I'm not mistaken, I was actually among the top three... but who's counting?" Though they were clearly the same age, Price affected an air that was considerably older; much like that of Kaiser Sorensen. He jutted his chin up a little higher to better look down on Sebastian. "And you're a music teacher at a local school here, right?"

Sebastian heard the condescension. He was used to it. "Yeah, you could say that." He wasn't about to give him the satisfaction of defending himself or his profession.

"I hear that it's a gratifying job." He glanced down at Sebastian's attire. "Though not a financially rewarding one, I take it."

Sebastian snorted in amusement as he realized he still wore the sweats Serena had loaned him.

"Slumming it this week, Bash," Kaiser said.

"I guess a week in the hospital can do that to a guy. I didn't take the time to change before coming over."

"Is it true you're working on a movie score?"

"Yeah, a Rick Steinberg production."

"I once knew a girl who was really a fan of yours. Despite her music choices, I still loved her. So I have you to thank for her endless entertainment when I had to travel. Go figure. I was never into all that mushy stuff. But, I guess a guy has to keep busy, right?"

146

"It certainly does keep me busy."

"You bet," Kaiser threw in. "He's so busy we have to make an appointment just to see him."

"Well then, I'll leave you to reconnect with your son, Mr. Sorensen." Price turned to Sebastian. "It was a pleasure meeting you, Bash."

The annoying nickname was barely tolerable from the likes of his mother and Willow, but on the lips of this man it was downright infuriating. Despite that, he grinned and nodded a salutation.

Price turned to Kaiser and offered a handshake. "Thank you once again, Mr. Sorensen, for you confidence in me."

"It's not idle confidence, Mr. Turnsby. Your track record speaks for itself. I have no doubt this new union will be a very profitable one." He patted Price on the shoulder as he led him to the elevator. "I'll have my lawyers draw up the necessary documents and send them to your place to be signed."

Price entered the elevator and shot Sebastian one last scrutinizing glance before the doors slid shut.

"What was that all about?" Sebastian said as he followed Kaiser into his office.

"I see you're feeling better."

Really? Now you want to talk about my health, Sebastian thought. "Much better."

"Good, good. I wanted to apologize on behalf of your mother. She desperately wanted to go see you at the hospital, but her commitment to everyone at the fundraiser…"

"I understand," Sebastian cut in. He didn't really want to hear all the excuses they could possibly come up with for not coming to see him.

"And as for me, well, you know how things pile up if I just miss a day at the office. Besides, I had this big deal with Price to finalize."

"So what *is* the deal with the Price guy?"

"He's just signed an agreement intending to purchase one of our subsidiaries… our line of Granite Gyms. Now I know talking business isn't what brought you here. What's on your mind, son?"

"I wanted to share with you the suspicions I have regarding my mysterious food poisoning."

"But your mother told me it wasn't food poisoning."

"Exactly."

"You suspect foul play?"

"D'you have any other suggestions?"

148

Kaiser stared blankly at him.

"In addition to that, I arrived at my place this morning and it'd been ransacked. Everything was overturned, every drawer emptied, even the contents of my refrigerator were on the floor."

"This whole episode with you in the hospital really brought home just how serious you and this new young lady are. I must say it came as a bit of a surprise." Kaiser chuckled. "I don't know if you'll succeed in getting your mother and Willow to back off, though, but good luck."

"First off, her name is Serena Singleton, not young lady." Sebastian couldn't believe he'd just brushed off the fact his place had been ransacked. "Secondly, did you hear what I just said?"

"Right, Serena. I knew her name had a lovely ring to it. A very efficient young woman. She's the one who kept us up to date on your condition."

"Dad…"

"Yes, yes. I heard you. Your place was ransacked. Apartments in your area are apt to be burglarized every now and then, despite the heavy security."

"This wasn't a burglary. Nothing was taken. They went in there looking for something."

"Assuming you're right, assuming someone went into your apartment looking for something, I think the best course of action at this moment is to keep it all under wraps."

"Seriously? I may have been intentionally poisoned and my place was broken into and you want to keep it hush hush? And what am I supposed to do? Just go on about my day as if nothing had happened?"

"Don't worry. I'll have someone look into it. Going to the police would just bring unwanted publicity to the whole situation. Your private issues should remain private. Bad press at this point in time could ruin this new deal."

Sebastian cocked a disbelieving brow. "Really? That's what concerns you? How all this will affect your new deal?"

"It's a multi-million dollar deal, son."

Sucking in an exasperated breath, Sebastian looked over his father's head at the grand view of Newport Harbor. He knew money and prestige were important to his father, but... this was too much. "Anyway, I just stopped by to see if you and Mom were all right. When I saw my apartment, I thought perhaps whoever had gone through my things might want to get to you two as well."

"We're fine, son."

"Apparently. As far as you're concerned, it never happened."

"Don't take it that way. You have to understand how this could affect more than just you. If it makes you feel better, I'll arrange for added security at your building. You should know by now that we can't let something like a nosy busybody get in the way of what needs to be done." He fumbled with a few files that lay on his desk. "To tell you the truth, I didn't really think you'd be targeted since you're so far removed from the business."

"Targeted?" His gut filled with dread. Not only was his father unmoved by the destruction of his own son's apartment, but he'd apparently anticipated some kind of trouble. "Are you telling me you were aware of some potential danger and you never said anything?"

"Like I said, son, I didn't think you'd be targeted."

"What's going on?"

"Nothing that concerns you."

"I beg to differ. I have a ransacked apartment that says different and, the last time I checked, I was still a part of this family."

Kaiser shoved his hands deep into his pant pockets and turned to look out at the ocean. "I didn't want to get you involved in this. I didn't want you to be troubled by..." He turned to face his son. "You know, I started this company from nothing, literally. Today it's a multi-billion dollar powerhouse and still you want nothing to do with it. I won't lie, I would have been the proudest father in the world if you'd chosen to follow in my footsteps; if you'd admired the company I'd built enough to come add your own blood, sweat and tears to the mix, but no... you had better things to do."

"You know I don't have a head for this sort of business."

"Your mother doesn't really have a head for business either, but she's nonetheless put great time and effort into hosting banquets, dinner parties, charitable events and everything in between. Even Willow and her mother take part. For crying out loud, Sebastian, you're my only child, my only son. You're

152

the sole heir to all this and..." He chocked and coughed into his fist. "Damn it, all you've done is turn your nose at us... at this." He spread his arms out, indicating his office.

"We've been through this before," Sebastian said in a monotone voice. "What is this trouble you're in? Why is security such an issue all of a sudden?"

"It's not really all of a sudden. It's part of the game. You have money and people want to get their hands on it. The more you have, the more ruthless they become. When your face appears on the front cover of Forbes with your net worth printed in big bold digits... well, it rattles people a bit. Seems everyone thinks they deserve a percentage of your success." Clearing his throat, he looked thoughtfully at his son. "When you were young, we were careful to keep you sheltered from it all; lunatics, kidnappers, the Lindbergh baby. Your mother wanted to make sure you were safe at all times. Despite many requests, we never allowed a photo of you to be published. But now... well, you're all grown up, and we thought you were safe. You're a strong and capable man, but I guess you're still vulnerable. People can go to ridiculous lengths when greed takes over."

Sebastian wanted to argue that his hadn't been a mere robbery, that money wasn't the issue, but his father firmly guided him out of his office.

"I know you probably don't believe me, but I'm truly happy to see you're better. You know, I'm still available if ever you want to set up a meeting to discuss your possible future here. There'll always be an office ready and waiting for you."

"Don't hold your breath." Sebastian managed a chuckle, but was far from amused.

"Well, I'm sure you have a lot to do today, what with cleaning up your place, so I'll let you get going."

Though being so politely dismissed, hurt the little boy inside, Sebastian stood straight and looked his father in the eye. "I wouldn't want to keep you from your obligations either, Dad." He shot him a curt salute and turned to head to the elevator. On the way he bumped into Darcy, his father's assistant.

"Sorry about that," Sebastian said as he realized he'd caused her to drop the stack of news she'd been carrying. He stooped down to help her.

"It's my fault. I'm in a hurry and…"

Neglecting to pick up every paper, Sebastian grabbed one copy and stared dumbfounded at it as he stood. The front page had a picture from the fundraiser. Though he sat at the table surrounded by his parents, Willow, her brother and mother, it was his arm around Serena that caught his eye. He was leaning close to her and the private smile she'd smiled just for him was now plastered on the front page for everyone to see.

The headline only made matters worse. "Has Sebastian Sorensen found someone else to woo?"

Silently berating himself for having risked the night out with her, he now realized it would be impossible for him to be involved with her on both a personal and professional level.

Chapter 12

Serena took a sip from her fifth cup of coffee and resumed pacing. Since talking to Sebastian she'd taken his suit out of her closet, put it back in, only to take it out again. She'd beaten a path from her living room to the kitchen and from there to her bedroom. She'd changed a half dozen times; shorts were too casual, a dress too contrived, yoga pants and sweater too laid back. She'd finally settled on a simple pair of jeans and a plain white t-shirt.

In vain she'd tried to sit down and relax, and had even turned on the television, but it was useless. She was agitated and nervous.

With a heavy thump she set down her cup of coffee. "That certainly isn't helping matters," she muttered.

For the hundredth time, she walked over to the window and looked out hoping to spot his car. She couldn't quite understand why she was so eager to see him again. Perhaps it was the past days spent at his bedside, wiping his brow, whispering encouraging

156

words in his ear and holding his hand through the night.

Of course she couldn't forget the numerous sponge baths she'd given him. Though she'd argued with the staff that she was in a better position to tend to such an intimate task, it quickly became clear as she sponged off his muscular chest and perfect body that it was a completely selfish endeavor. She wanted to be close to him, to touch him, to see him, to give him pleasure without him even knowing it… and she did. It was her own guilty pleasure. Whatever it is about Sebastian Sorensen, she found herself wanting and willing to be very naughty with him.

Then again there was that smooth and sexy voice when he'd called to tell her he was on his way. Even over the phone his silky voice was enough to make her melt. She wanted to steel herself for the encounter to come. In her imaginary rehearsals she was cool and collected when he passed by to pick up his suit. She didn't fawn or blush. She didn't stutter or blunder.

But when the moment came, the moment he walked through that door, how would she be like?

The doorbell rang and her heart immediately did a flip. Before opening the door, she took in three long, deep breaths and smiled, radiantly. "Hi, Sebastian."

He'd barely had time to step into her apartment than she rushed into his arms. She felt him stiffen for a surprised moment before wrapping his arms around her.

"I'm so happy to see you. You sounded so strange when I called you. I was worried about you." Serena suddenly felt the need to justify her move. As she'd feared, her cool and collected self flew out the window the moment his hot and sexy self entered her apartment. He was dressed in black from head to toe, which brought out the inky black of his tresses and made his blue eyes more piercing. His upper body muscles were outlined perfectly against the soft silky shirt so smooth, she wanted to rub her cheeks against the fabric. She could hardly believe she'd thrown herself into his arms.

But as she tried to back away from him, he held her steady, his hands resting on top of her hips, close to the top of her jeans. It was familiar, yet heated at the same time, sending little shocks of heat through her, and making her nipples stand at alert. "It's good to know *somebody* worries about me." Sebastian's eyes looked deeply into hers before moving down to her shirt, her breasts, and back up to her face.

Her heart instantly went out to him. She knew his parents' indifference affected him more than he let on. "I've invested a lot of time in your wellbeing," she said with a lighthearted chuckle. "You know I was at the hospital all week." She felt the heat of the moment and sought to cool it with humor, but his warm hands remained on her waist, reminding her just how much she wanted to be touched by him.

"Well, I hope you get a satisfactory return on that investment." His voice was low, almost a growl, while his eyes smoldered with insinuation as he pulled her closer until her crotch was up against the front of his pants. Feeling his hardness, she knew the attraction was mutual. Remembering how well-endowed he was while giving him a sponge bath, her face flamed with want and the need to explore him.

The heat of her cheeks became intolerable and she pulled away. "I'll go get your suit," she murmured as she headed to her bedroom closet. In the privacy of her room, she batted her hand in front of her face in an attempt to cool her cheeks. The effect he had on her surpassed any experience she'd ever had and she didn't know how to respond.

Concentrating on the task at hand, she pulled the suit out of the closet and turned to head back to Sebastian only to find him in the doorway, his eyes narrow with lust.

"Ah, yes… the suit," he said. "I knew I had another reason for coming here."

Serena cocked her head to the side. "Another reason? What's the first?"

"Honestly? The first is just to see you again."

"You saw me this morning, silly. Don't try to tell me that we saw each other a few hours ago and you already miss me."

"You're right, and I won't insult your intelligence by trying to tell you I missed you, however, that doesn't mean I didn't look forward to seeing you again." He took his suit from her and hooked it on the doorknob. "Truth be told, there is another reason that brings me here."

Her gut tightened as she anticipated his next words. She remembered the tension that'd been in his voice when she'd called him that morning. That same tension was there again.

"I had an unexpected surprise when I arrived at my place."

"Oh?"

He led her to her bed and sat her down. "Someone broke in and went through my things."

Shocked into silence, Serena simply stared up at him.

"I don't know what they were looking for, but…"

"You're a rich guy. It could…"

"It wasn't a burglary." Taking her hands in his, he sat beside her.

"Um, okay."

"There's more."

She didn't even want to ask.

"I stopped by my father's office… just to make sure he was okay… that my mom was okay."

"And?"

"They're surprisingly fine. Nothing fazes them, apparently. My father, in addition to being unmoved by my week in the hospital, was utterly unperturbed by the break in."

"That's hard to believe."

"I'll agree with you there, but I quickly learned why he was so unperturbed. He's been anticipating something like this for a while."

"Something like what?"

"Hmph." He shrugged as his eyes became shadowed with anger. "I don't really know. Something about protecting me all these years. Something about being old enough to take care of myself now. He didn't really divulge much."

"Are you afraid something else will happen?"

Averting her gaze, he swallowed. The anger left his eyes as worry and concern took its place.

"What is it?" she said as her gut tightened again.

He reached into the pocket of the jeans he wore and pulled out the front page of a newspaper. "Apparently we're already an item."

Serena tried to read his intended meaning as she looked at the photo. "I don't get it. What are you saying?"

"I'm worried for your safety."

She bolted off the bed and turned to stare down at him. "Me? Why? What did I do?"

162

"You were seen with me." Reaching up to take her hand, he pulled her closer. "I'm so sorry. I should've never invited you to that dinner. Not only did I bore you to tears, but now…"

"Don't be silly." Though she wanted to reassure him, her voice was oddly dead. "I had a wonderful time."

He laughed off her comment. "Nice try. Look, I've already arranged for additional security here. I just have to check with the superintendent to make sure they'll allow it."

His concern for her did quick work of her growing fear. Wanting to sooth the fear she now saw in his eyes, she brought her hand to his cheek. Her vision blurred as tears welled up. I appreciate your concern, but I think I'll be okay. Security here is already pretty decent."

He brought his hand over hers and pressed it to his cheek then turned to kiss the palm of her hand, sending shivers through her. His tender gesture was a surprise, as well as his concern for her. "Pretty decent isn't enough." His hands snaked around her waist and he pulled her closer, pressing his face into her chest.

The touch of his hands was electrifying and she longed to get closer still. Her hands found refuge in his thick mass of hair and Sebastian growled his pleasure as she raked her nails along his scalp, holding him to her bosom as she did so. His growls turned to sighs of contentment while his arms tightened their hold on her.

"I'd spend the day getting lost in you," he murmured, hungrily.

So would I, Serena mused. So would I.

She looked down at him and kissed his brow.

His hands found their way under her shirt and his fingers burned her skin. She wanted him and knew she wouldn't be able to hold back much longer. Her body was hungry for a man and he was perfect in every way.

Her lips trailed down his temple to his cheek. Anticipation of finding his lips overwhelmed her and her knees turned to mush. She leaned into him, inadvertently pushing him back onto the bed. His strong grip on her wrists brought her down over him and his kiss came swiftly and was more passionate than she had expected, devouring her with his mouth. Her head swirled in desire and for a long moment of complete abandon, she was barely aware of her surroundings. The touch of his hands on her skin, the softness of his lips over hers and the moist sweetness of his tongue were all that mattered. It was too easy to get lost in his hold and she didn't want to have to think of when and how she'd regain control.

Their lips left each other when Sebastian pushed her off him and held her aloft with one hand while his other hand worked to free her of her t-shirt. Not wanting to be outdone, she sat back and pulled him into a seated position and quickly unbuttoned his shirt until he was bare chested in front of her, and she was running her hands over his magnificent body.

An erotic sigh escaped her as her eyes remained riveted to the perfect biceps that faced her. Smooth and soft skin pulled taunt over strong and perfectly shaped muscles was more than she could resist. Her hands fluttered up to touch his chest then tickled their way down over every ab while her mouth went straight to his chest where she stuck out her tongue to lick his nipple. He groaned before pulling her face up to kiss her deeply, while his hands reached under her bra to begin rubbing her nipples in circular motions that made her want to jump out of her skin. "That," he growled into her ear, "is for licking me

before I gave you permission. It. Was. Very. Naughty."
He pulled up her shirt and her bra at the same time
before plunging down his face to grab hold of her
nipple in his mouth. When his teeth lightly grazed it,
she moaned in pleasure. Her back arched as she jutted
her breasts out further towards his hungry mouth,
while his tongue began circling each nipple, making
her shudder with each lick. "That's for being naughty,
not nice, Miss Singleton." He sucked in her breast,
while his hand plunged into the front of her jeans,
reaching to her sensitive clit to begin rubbing.

"Oh, Sebastian," Serena cried.

"Do you intend on asking me for permission to
touch or lick my nipples from now on?" Sebastian
asked.

"If I don't?" Serena asked, breathlessly.

"Then there's more punishment like this to
come, only I won't let you have the satisfaction of
coming."

Serena's eyes opened wide, and she said,
"That's torturous alright, Sebastian. I can't imagine not
being able to…"

"Hush," Sebastian said gently, "I won't punish
you so harshly. It will be all sweetness, like this," he

plunged his fingers into her, while his thumb continued to rub at her clit, causing her to writhe against him. The pressure within her was mounting so quickly, she was going to come if he continued on with his pleasurable onslaught.

Right before she thought she wasn't going to hold onto her control any further, he pulled his fingers out, before licking them, causing her to shudder slightly. "You taste just as sweet as I imagined you'd be, Serena." He smiled as he leaned into her, "Deliciously feminine, yet wild, like a vintage wine." He kissed her. "You don't even know how exquisite you are."

Exquisite? Sebastian Sorensen thought she was exquisite? If she was exquisite, then he must be vintage. She had to have a taste of him. Overwhelmed with the erotic images that played in her mind, she kissed him harder and plunged her tongue into the depths of his mouth. His lips tasted so good, she wondered if she'd ever get enough.

In the distance the doorbell rang, but she refused to acknowledge it. She didn't want the moment to end. She didn't want to stray from the heat of his body and she didn't want his fingers to stop their journey over her skin. He'd unfastened the button of her jeans and was working the zipper down when he suddenly stopped.

"I think you have a visitor," Sebastian said with annoying efficiency. With hot and gentle hands, he pried her off him.

Flustered beyond comprehension, she pushed her hair off her face and stared dumbfounded at him. How could he remain so cool and unmoved in such a heated moment?

"I'm not expecting anyone." She heard the strange huskiness in her voice and realized just how badly she wanted to remain in the moment. Whoever was at the door would leave. It couldn't possibly be important. It couldn't possibly be more important than this.

"I think it might be your superintendent. I gave him a call about the security issue with the building." Sebastian stood and pulled the black shirt back on. "He said he'd drop by if he had the chance."

Security? Serena could almost feel the tears of frustration working their way to her eyes. Instead of allowing that emotion to take over, she pulled her t-shirt and bra down and went to open the door all the while averting Sebastian's gaze. She didn't want him to see just how frustrated she was by this untimely interruption.

He grabbed her wrist and stopped her progress. "Don't look so disappointed," he whispered, before kissing her thoroughly, making her knees crumble as she melted into him. "This isn't over." He took the lead and opened the door.

"You the one who called about the security?" Mr. Hough said. He was a short and stout man who had little time to lose and made sure everyone knew it.

"Yes, I am." Sebastian opened the door wider and gestured for Mr. Hough to enter. "Come sit down."

Serena nodded a quick greeting at the super. She'd only met once or twice before, but had never spoken to him.

"No need to sit," Mr. Hough said. "We already have a contract with a security guy. He takes care of the buzzers, doors, windows and all that stuff. We used to have a camera out back. We could see what went on in the parking lot, but that got busted last year and we never replaced it."

"Is there a possibility of replacing it now?"

"The contract runs for another year," Mr. Hough said with a shake of his head. "Not much I can do now to change that."

"Sure, I understand." Sebastian took a step forward, ready to close the door.

Mr. Hough turned to look at Serena. "If you're really concerned about a break in or whatever, I can add a chain to your door; maybe a deadbolt."

"I've got it from here on in," Sebastian said. "Thanks anyway."

"No problem."

Sebastian shut the door and leaned into it. "I guess I'll have to take your security into my own hands."

Serena liked the sound of that.

"Now, where were we?" Sebastian asked, moving towards her while unbuttoning his shirt.

Serena wanted so badly to continue where they left off before the superintendent arrived, but she stepped back. As much as she wanted Sebastian, she had to hold back before it went any further. She needed to make sure she got an adviser, and she needed Sebastian to take her seriously. "Not so fast,

Professor," Serena said. "We don't have to rush into anything, and…"

"You still want me as an adviser," Sebastian said. He ran his fingers through his hair before letting out a frustrated growl. "I guess we'll have to settle that one way or another. Meet me at my office on campus tomorrow after I have a chance to talk to the officials, and I'll let you know where we stand."

Serena nodded, as Sebastian gathered his things, heading towards the door.

"If you excuse me, I'll have to go. Staying here with you one minute longer will guarantee me ravaging you on the spot so I'll see you tomorrow. Remember to lock your doors, and don't let anyone you don't know in."

"Yes, mother," Serena joked, but deep down inside, she wanted him to stay. And to ravage her as he promised.

Sebastian smiled and left.

Chapter 13

Serena felt a heated blush come to her cheeks the moment she approached the door to Sebastian's office. Though she'd come to see him on official business, her body wasn't quite in tune to what her head was planning; getting Sebastian to sign the documents that would officially declare him her adviser.

When he opened the door, she fought the incredible impulse to push him to the wall and throw herself all over him, to continue where they left off. Though the sight of him in her old sweatshirt hadn't diminished his appeal, seeing him now in a proper suit and tie definitely had a strong effect on her.

"You managed to make it a few minutes early this time," Sebastian teased.

"Well, I expect to officially have an advisor today, so…"

"Yeah." He seemed distracted as he returned behind his desk, sat down and idly fiddled with a pen. "I wanted to talk to you about that."

"I know. That's why I'm here." She sat in the seat across from him and tried to ignore his odd behavior. She wanted to remain upbeat. This was the day everything would get settled, but she was struck with a sinking feeling.

"Serena." His tone was stony, almost cold.

Her upbeat disposition took another hit and she bit her lip. What was wrong now?

"I don't think I can be your adviser."

"What?" She shot out of her seat and pounded her fist to his desk. "No! You can't do this."

Holding out a calming hand, he gestured for her to sit back down. "You don't have to shout, Serena. Just hear me out."

"No, I won't hear you out." She ignored his request to sit back down. "Have you been stringing me along? You think you can just toy with me... I went to that damn party and..."

"Serena!" He came around his desk and rushed toward her.

For a moment she thought he was going to physically throw her out of his office, but he grabbed her by the arms and roughly pulled her to him. Taken aback she resisted a second, but he persisted and held

173

her close. In an instant his lips were over hers and while she melted into him, her head spun with confusion. What was he doing to her?

"This is what I want," Sebastian muttered through his kisses. "I want to hold you, to touch you, to kiss you. I want your body against mine. I want to plunge myself deep into you so badly and give you multiple orgasms, while making the most exquisite love you'll ever experience."

"So do I," she whispered. "But…"

He pulled away and looked at her. "While I'd be honored to be your adviser, Serena, I'd much prefer to be your lover."

She gasped and her eyes widened with shock.

"I can't be both," Sebastian went on. "Serena, we've only seen each other a few times and each time has been torture. I have to control myself from grabbing you, ripping off your clothes, and throwing you up against the wall or on my desk and fuck the hell out of you. I know I'm not the only one to feel the chemistry between us, right?"

"Okay, you're right, but, as much as…" She hesitated. She didn't want to come straight out and admit just how much she'd enjoy having him as her

174

lover. "My music is very important to me, Sebastian. Yes, I'm drawn to you. You're a very charismatic man, and…" Damn how she would enjoy having him as her lover. She can feel his fingers inside of her while his teeth lightly graze her nipples still from yesterday's encounter when he came over to see her about security. Darn, was he an amazing lover. Just his kiss was enough to make her wet with want. And he was a generous doting lover. He took great care to make sure she was enjoying herself more than he did. She took a deep breath. "But I need an adviser."

"And you really think we could just work together, side by side, spending so much time together without ever…?" He eyed her with lusty intent, and pulled her against him, brushing her crotch against his hardness. She sucked in some air at the touch. "Dammit, Serena. I can't even be in the same room with you without getting a massive hard-on. How can I work with you side by side without wanting to spend all my time bending you over, lifting your skirt, and taking you from behind? How can I resist tearing off your clothes and going down on you, so I can taste you. My hunger for you is insatiable, Serena. You've unleashed a side of me that I can barely control. I can't get enough of you." He plunged his tongue inside her mouth, tangling it with hers to emphasize how thoroughly he wanted her.

Lost in their heated kiss, she moaned, melting into his broad chest, wanting his strong arms around her, protecting her, wanting her. She knew he was right, but she refused to admit it. Dammit, she needed an adviser. It was her dream to become a composer, in a field where there were hardly any women. "Look," she pulled away a little shakily. "A little abstinence never killed anyone." With every word that slipped off her tongue, she knew how ridiculous it sounded.

Sebastian pulled her closer and pressed his pelvis to hers. "Really?"

"Um." The temperature in the room was suddenly suffocating. "Sebastian, I just think…"

He kissed her, deep and long, and any notion of music, composition or advisers flew out the window.

"I have a colleague," Sebastian said when he pulled back. "He would be the perfect adviser for you. He's in his sixties, a grandfather, and much more experienced than I am in churning out the next generation of music composition talent. If need be, I could be second in line, but, to tell you the truth, I don't think I'd get much advising done where you're concerned."

An excited thrill shot through her. "I guess I could live with that arrangement, but…" Her mind left the heated bed she'd share with him and returned to the career she had in mind… the future she had in store. "Who's your colleague? Is he as renowned as you?"

"Not quite." Sebastian smiled and seemed flustered for the first time. "I appreciate your confidence in me. I guess amidst all this I could still help you with your studies, just not officially."

"But you just said you couldn't…"

Chuckling, he snuggled his nose into the crook of her neck. "I think I'll be able to get control of myself enough to write beautiful music with you…naked or in the bathtub or both."

"So, you'd still advise me."

"Informally, I can still teach you, and you can be my secret protégé. It'd be the best of both worlds. I could teach you in all kinds of composition while also giving you an education in receiving and giving intense pleasure. It would also solve the whole issue with the security at your building."

"How's that?"

"Oh, didn't I mention... I'd like to have you stay at my place. That way I could keep an eye on you... in every way."

"Your place?"

"Yes."

"Us together?"

"Yes."

"I don't know..."

"I do."

"I want to say yes..." This wasn't what she'd planned and she couldn't help but wonder how her relationship with him would pan out. What if it became disastrous? What if after a few weeks he tired of her, got bored with her and wanted to move on? What would happen to her music then? What would happen to everything? "As tempted as I am, Sebastian..."

"Okay, think about it."

"Sebastian."

"Go home, take a good long bath with a nice glass of wine and think it all over. Think about me, about us, about your music and about the best choice you can make at this point in time. If you choose to have me strictly as your adviser, stay home tonight and come back to my office tomorrow morning, wearing something godawfully prim and proper, maybe even a knight's armor or a chastity belt. If you choose to become my protégé and have me as your lover, your protector, your mentor and your adviser, come to me tonight… at my place."

***

Her bath only heightened the desire that had built up all day. Serena knew Sebastian was right. If he were to become her adviser, their attraction to one another was bound to complicate things. If she was to have the older gentleman as her adviser and Sebastian as her secret mentor and adviser with all the benefits of being a lover, she can have the best of both worlds. She can still have Sebastian Sorensen in both ways without giving him up at all. She didn't think she could at this moment. She took another sip of wine and tried to find another argument. There was none. Despite having been so pragmatic and studious over the past year, she knew little work would get done if he were to be constantly on her mind.

Secretly, she was pleased with herself. She'd come to a decision even if half her brain continued the debating process.

The next hour flew by as she soaked in the fragrant bath water and relaxed while enjoying the titillating excitement of anticipation. With the bath water almost cold, she got out, dried off and got dressed. Without wasting too much time she picked out her favorite flower print summer dress then quickly grabbed a few of her favorite items and shoved them in a suitcase.

Within the next hour she was at Sebastian's door.

"I knew you'd come," he said simply, his blue eyes intensely fastened to hers.

Serena set her suitcase on the floor and for a strangely tense moment they stared at each other.

"I want you to feel at home." Sebastian picked up the suitcase and brought it into his bedroom.

"I'll admit this feels a little strange." Serena took in her new surroundings as she followed him.

"It'll pass."

"I've been living alone for a long time, and..."

"So have I. I think I can handle the adjustment."

Acutely aware of the large bed just a few feet away, Serena felt the molten heat work its way up her legs only to bubble over where her thighs met.

Sebastian set her suitcase down and proceeded to open the large walk in closet. "I thought it might be a good idea to sacrifice half my closet space."

Every girl's dream; a huge closet with more than enough room to hang her entire wardrobe and then some, but right now, her wardrobe and its future habitat were the last things on her mind. Her hands twitched with nervous energy. How long was he going to torture her like this?

"You even have room for several pairs of shoes," he went on.

"That's really nice of you." *But can we move on to more… intimate discussions?*

"I hope you like chicken."

"I beg your pardon."

"For dinner. I thought we could have dinner together, discuss our… living arrangement." The smile he offered her was wicked and wild. It was irresistible.

181

When are you going to kiss me? she wanted to shout. She was already wet with anticipation.

"How 'bout a glass of wine? Red or white?" He headed for the door.

"Neither." Serena reached out to take his hand.

"Hungry?" He cocked a knowing brow.

Her head involuntarily tilted forward in a nod while her fingers played along the back of his hand.

He gripped her fingers and pulled her closer. Licking his lips he looked intently at her. "I was hoping you'd be." Cupping her cheeks he kissed her hard and passionately, his steps strong and powerful as he backed her to the bed.

She fell back, willingly, hungrily wanting to feel his body against hers. But before allowing her that pleasure, he stood looking down at her. His eyes passed over every inch of her. They lingered on her legs and skimmed up high on her thighs that'd been left exposed when the skirt of her dress had followed her fall.

"You're a beautiful creature, Serena." Sebastian slowly unbuttoned every button of his shirt. "You're soft and gentle and kind, yet..." He bit his lip as he opened his shirt to expose his chest.

It was difficult to concentrate on his words as Serena took in the sight of him.

"Yet I sense there's a fire. You smolder and..." He bared his shoulders, his biceps, his torso. "It makes for an intriguing combination. That innocent flame. That naïve, slow burning amber." He let the shirt fall to the floor and worked on the fastenings of his slacks.

Flame, yes. She felt it burning with an intensity that was about to drive her mad. Her breasts felt heavy with longing and her nipples were hard with anticipation. Her thighs tingled with wanting and she pressed them tightly together hoping to alleviate the sensation, but it only made matters worse. She licked her lips and tried to control the heavy breaths that shook her chest.

Sebastian let his slacks drop to the floor and Serena sat up to face the bulge in the tight, white boxer briefs. He was such a magnificent specimen of a man. Every muscle was toned, and his skin just lightly bronzed by the sun.

She brought a finger to the hem of his boxer briefs and was rewarded with a hungry sigh. Her own groan of anticipation met his sigh as her finger sneaked under the white cotton and touched his burning skin.

The bulge, pure in its white dressing, pounded like an excited heartbeat. Sebastian grasped her hand and pulled it away from him. "Not so fast." With his free hand he reached for one of the thin straps that held her dress up and let it fall off her shoulder, leaving the fabric of her dress just barely clinging to her breast. "I want to take a good look at you."

Serena kept her eyes on his, pleased with the appreciation she saw reflected in them. He licked his lips and let his finger follow the line of fabric now draped over her breast. As his finger circled the orb, liberating it from the fragile fabric and exposing it to the air, to his sight and to his touch, Serena felt a surge of moisture collect between her thighs.

With agonizingly slow motions, he freed her other breast, letting her dress pool around her waist. "You certainly played a nasty trick on me that first day, arriving all covered up, yet I knew, when I peeled away the layers, I'd find the beauty and perfection I now see." In unison, his hands weighed her breasts. "You have such perfect breasts. So soft and supple." His touch was delicate and unhurried as he softly and reverently touched every part of her breasts until she was screaming to have him take them into his mouth.

184

Maintaining control of her breathing was now impossible. Her chest rose and fell with every heavy breath. She longed to arch her back and press her breasts into his hands. For an interminable minute his fingers played along the outer reaches of her breasts, heightening her desire to have him take a stronger hold, to pinch a nipple, to suckle.

His eyes darkened and took on a wicked gleam. He took great pleasure in taunting her; that much she could see. His fingers stopped their play on her breasts. Her lips parted in anticipation of his next move.

"I want to please you," he said in a voice so deep and husky, she barely recognized it. Cupping her breasts, he brought his thumbs to her nipples and she let out a gasp of surprise and pleasure. "Does this please you?"

"Yes," she breathed.

Releasing her breasts all too quickly, he knelt before her and gently pushed the remainder of her skirt up to join the bodice of her dress. "I want to see for myself just how much you enjoy this." With his index finger, he drew a line along the edge of her pale blue panties.

She inhaled a trembling breath and Sebastian looked at her. "Tell me, Serena," he said, his voice like dark, hot honey on her name. "Do you want me for your lover?"

Every inch of her body, every nerve ending wanted to shout out her response. She wanted him. She'd known she'd wanted him from the moment she'd first met him, but now... that want, that desire was all consuming. Not trusting her voice, she nodded.

His finger snaked under her panties and found the source of moisture. "If you've had a change of heart, we can stop this right now... before we go too far."

The light touch of his finger already had her on the edge of profound pleasure.

"Perhaps my touch isn't what you'd hoped for. Perhaps I'm not as agile as you'd thought. If you think I'd be better suited to simply be your adviser, it's not too late." He pulled aside the narrow panel of her panties and looked at the working of his index finger. "It's not too late," he whispered.

Her breath caught in her throat. Any moment now she would explode. He taunted her by circling the nub of sensitive nerve endings with his finger.

"What do you want, Serena?" As his finger continued its slow torture, his warm breath brushed her breast.

"You," she groaned.

"Are you certain?"

"Yes."

Simultaneously, he brought his lips and tongue over one aching nipple while his finger, drenched in moisture, made one simple move over the sensitive nerve endings that beckoned his touch.

With a loud cry of rapture, Serena let her body take over. Her fingers raked through his thick hair and pulled him to her breasts. She pulled down his boxers, grabbing hold of his thick shaft that was hard and ready for her. "Please," she cried.

"Please what?" Sebastian asked.

"Please, lover, make me come. I can't stand it any longer."

Sebastian smiled a wicked smile before he ripped off her panties, pulled over a drawer full of condoms, tore off the wrappings to place one on and hovered over her. "Do I have your permission to take you?"

"Yes," she said. "As much as possible. Teach me how to be passionate, show me what it can be like."

"Then I aim to teach," he plunged hard and fast into her, rocking her clit and hitting her spot simultaneously sending her eyes to widen and clench her teeth in the intense pleasure she felt. Then slowly he made his way out, before plunging into her again, hitting her exactly where her spot was while taking his fingers to work her clit. She clenched her teeth but let out a loud guttural moan that shook her to the core. He pulled out slowly and began rhythmically pumping her in and out hitting her spot each time while filling every crevice of her with pleasure. He was in total control, passionate, and sensual, knowing exactly when to add pressure, get sensitive, be gentle, and when to get wild.

After flipping her around and taking her from behind, his hands covering her breasts while he entered her and pumped her rhythmically, twisting his hips to take her deeper, she couldn't hold on any longer. "I'm going to..."

"Hold on a little bit longer, baby," he said, kissing and then biting her nipple. "I'll come with you." He flipped her on top of him while he laid on his back and began moving her hips against him, his shaft buried deep within her. "Ride me, Serena," he said. "Let loose that passion of yours. You have it within, you know, that temper, that energy. Let it all out on me now."

Serena began going up and down on him, wriggling her hips as she slid him in and out, making him groan as she increased her pace and began touching him at the base. She felt the tension mounting within her, felt his body shake, and when he reached up with his hips to pump her from beneath, she couldn't hold on. Shaking with ecstasy, her body exploded with pleasure and with the desire for more, as he let out a groan that shook her deeper, "Serena baby, you're mine." He pulled her to him, kissing her on the lips and on the temples before holding her tight like a cherished woman. "You're all mine."

Chapter 14

Serena awoke to a steaming cup of coffee set on the bedside table. In a long, narrow vase beside it was a single magenta rose. It was sweet and thoughtful, but didn't make up for the empty bed. Though her night with Sebastian had been as sleepless and sweaty as every other night of the past two weeks, she longed to touch him again.

Jacked up on an elbow, she took a quick sniff of the rose then took a sip of coffee. These past days Sebastian had proven to be as good a lover as cook. Still nude, still glistening with sweat, she sat up and smiled at the thought of the heated and passionate nights she'd shared with him every night since she became his protégé. He was insatiable, and when it came to him, she couldn't get enough, too.

A quick glance down at her thighs and she was reminded of the hunger he'd displayed the night before. After a long evening at the university, he'd arrived late and had found her laboring over a new composition.

The moment he walked through the door, she knew what he wanted. She'd prepared for it.

With a limited wardrobe, she'd decided to raid his side of the closet. A crisp white button down shirt went perfectly with the black lace thong she'd pulled on. She'd only buttoned the middle four buttons and had wrapped an exquisite black tie about her neck. It hung invitingly between her breasts, naughty and alluring. In contrast, she'd pulled her hair up into a bun.

The finishing touch; four inch black heels that glistened in the candlelight.

"I'm sure Wolfgang never had it so good," Sebastian said the moment he spotted her. He kicked off his shoes and whipped off his tie.

"I think Wolfgang would have hit his head against the wall if he'd had me for a student. I've barely written two bars."

"Your academic endeavors weren't really what I was referring to."

Serena left her writing and stood to face her mentor. "Oh?" Twirling her pen innocently, she looked at him, wide eyed, while her fingers played with the tie against her bare chest.

"I'd always thought my every day professor garb was rather boring and drab." He took her hand and held it up as he inspected her. "On you, however... Wow."

"Well, you've barely let me out of the house since I moved in, so I'm getting a little low on clean clothes."

"Looking the way you do, I happily give you permission to go through my closet as much as you like... Any time."

"So, you like?" She tossed her pen on the table.

He reached for the tie, the back of his hand brushing against her breast. "I think this is going to be my favorite tie from now on." His eyes gleamed with mischief.

"Good." Serena looked at him, aroused by the hunger she saw in his eyes. They'd made love countless times that week, yet he still hungered for her as much as he had that first night. She'd feared he'd tire of her after a few heated nights, but it just got better and better. He was insatiable, and when it came to him, she was just as hungry.

Wrapping the tie around his fist, Sebastian pulled her to him and unpinned her hair, letting it fall

192

in waves about her shoulders. "Do you know how impossible it is to survive a day at the university when all I want is to…?" Mischief turned to lust as his eyes narrowed and his lips curved into a hungry sneer.

She'd seen that look before. It'd been strange, even frightening at first, but she'd come to enjoy what followed. Every time she'd seen that expression she'd felt as though Sebastian had vacated his body, leaving his limbs to act on pure instinct.

His instinct, animal, wild, almost ferocious, was delicious.

He gave the tie a forceful yank that propelled her forward. She smashed into his chest, but before she could reach out to touch him, he yanked her back away from him. Releasing the tie, he grabbed each panel of the shirt and tore it apart, sending buttons flying across the room.

Though her breasts weren't completely exposed, the ferocious animal he'd become stared down at the skin he'd bared. She stood staring at him, waiting for his next move. He'd proven to be so unpredictable over the course of the two weeks; quiet and loving one night, hard, outrageous and wild the next. He was as complicated a lover as he was the musician. Moody, loving, and passionate like his music.

Taking a firm hold of the tie once more, he pulled her backward until she hit the ceiling to floor glass panel that overlooked the city.

"I want to show the world the treasure I've found," he growled. He spun her around and pushed her to the window.

With one hand pressed to the middle of her back he held her in place. Her breasts pressed against the cold glass as he worked to rid himself of his pants. Aside from a vague reflection of him in the window at the far wall, she couldn't see what he was doing, but she heard his every move.

His grunts were hot and impatient... not to mention promising. A leathery swish sounded as he pulled his belt off. It landed several feet away from them with a light clink. The zipper trumpeted its descent followed by the ruffle of fabric pooling on the floor.

Leaning into her, he pulled her shirt off one shoulder and released a portion of his aggression by biting into the firm flesh. She bit her lip as his teeth brought exquisite pain and his lips the reward of a warm, soothing balm.

"I want to show you the pleasure…" His hand snaked around her waist, over her belly and up to take a firm grip of a breast. He took a sip of cold ice water before he pinched her nipple to the point of pain. Then soothing it with his cool mouth. His teeth and cold lips continued to play over her shoulder, up her neck, stopping at her ear, sending pleasurable sensations up and down her skin.

With a forceful thrust, he pushed himself into her, pressing his hardness against her buttocks. "How hot are you for me, Serena?"

"Look for yourself," she dared.

Sebastian reached in front of her and roughly pulled her thighs apart. His fingers delved deep within the folds of moisture and heat. "Pretty damn hot." Serena let out a deep rooted groan that reverberated against the glass. Her breath fogged the window and dampened her cheek.

Sebastian pushed her breasts against the glass, her nipples outlined clearly in the frosted window for all the world to see, while he removed the rest of his clothing, discarding it on the ground. From behind, he pushed into her folds hard and then slowly, eliciting a low moan from deep within her. "Oh Sebastian."

Sebastian pulled out and thrust slowly, filling her again in response. She cried out, but Sebastian turned her around, capturing her mouth and cry in his as he devoured her mouth and licked his way down to her breasts and nipples. "Nothing sexier than seeing a woman's naked breasts pressed up against the window, Serena. Except this." He lifted Serena until she was sitting on his shoulders, and his mouth was buried into her folds, lapping her up as he braced his hips and knees against the window, his buttocks clenched, all muscles tight.

Serena threw her head back, as she clawed at Sebastian's back. She can imagine how incredibly hot he looked fully naked against the window, all his muscles on display, and she shuddered, along with the intense buildup of Sebastian's tongue on her. When her shuddering subsided, she murmured, "I want to show the world a Sebastian Sorensen rarely seen."

Sebastian smiled. "What do you have in mind?"

"You up against the window. Me in front." Serena licked her lips.

"I like how that sounds," Sebastian said. "What do you…" his sentence stopped in mid-air as Serena surprised him by gripping his shaft and mounting him, wrapping her legs around his waist. "Serena…" he groaned.

Serena clenched tightly as she climbed Sebastian, causing him to inhale and shudder. "Sebastian…"

He lifted her higher, capturing her hands in his, kissing her on her breasts and stomach while lowering her down. She was falling down on top of him when he pushed up, slamming her against him and against the window. He leaned forward, whispering into her ears, while fogging up the glass with his hot breath. "For that little surprise…" he thrust into her, "you deserve…" he thrust harder, causing her to ride up the window, her butt wiping away the fog on the window, "No mercy," he thrust deeper and faster still until she grabbed onto his soft wavy hair, clenching it into her hands, and moaning deep into his neck as she came so hard, her body crumpled on top of him. Seconds later, he let out a cry and pulled her tight against him, climaxing against her.

Both glistening from sweat and heat from each other, they sagged against the window, still wrapped around each other unable to let go.

Serena smiled now as she took her cup of coffee and felt the pain of his fingers on her thighs. That brief moment of pain and the pale blue marks that remained were well worth the exquisite night of love making that had followed.

"Enough of wallowing in sexual bliss," she snapped at herself as she got out of bed. "We've got a composition to work on."

Barefoot and still wearing his shirt, she headed to the kitchen. A bowl of fresh fruit was set on the granite counter, beside it, a note.

My vixen,

I'm sure you already know just how happy I am with our living arrangement. These past nights have far exceeded my expectations. They've also made me a little forgetful when it comes to my other obligations.

I was rudely reminded of that this morning when I awoke to a call reprimanding me for not be where I had said I'd be; a meeting in Seattle.

Two, three days at the most and I should be back home, in your bed, in your arms.

Please forgive my hasty departure… Keep our bed warm until I return.

Yours,

Sebastian

Smiling, she brought the handwritten note to her chest. As rough and tough as he could get during lovemaking, which she loved as much as he did, he proved to be sweet and tender outside the bedroom.

With him gone, his place felt empty and cold and she suddenly longed to get out. Munching on a chunk of pineapple she went in search of her phone and called Laura.

"Well, hallelujah. I thought I'd never hear from you again," Laura exclaimed.

"Sorry. I'm drowning under works, compositions and more work." Serena gulped down a sip of coffee. "But I'm free today and I think I'm getting cabin fever. What are you up to?"

"I had a few things to pick up at the store, grab lunch, maybe a little idle shopping."

"Sounds perfect."

Four hours later they arrived at Laura's apartment, their arms weighed down with a dozen bags. Shoes, skirts, lingerie, dresses, panties and more.

"You never shop like this. What's up?" They set the bags down by the door and Laura made a beeline for the mini wine cellar under the kitchen counter.

"What do you mean? I like to shop when I get a chance."

"Serena, I've known you long enough to know you can be a rather pragmatic shopper. You never buy what you don't need. Today you practically bought out that boutique." She popped open a bottle of Chardonnay and poured them each of glass.

"I've been bogged down with music, music and more music." Serena took her glass of wine and took a delicate sip. "I just needed to get out and surround myself with new stuff. I needed to think about something else."

"Why do I get the feeling you're not telling me the whole story?" Laura led the way to the big cushy sofa in the living room and sat down.

"Okay, maybe... but it's too soon to talk about it. I don't want to jinx it." She sat down and took a big gulp of wine. Though she longed to talk about her relationship to Sebastian, she wasn't quite ready to put it out there. She'd been shoving back deep inside her the growing emotions that'd built up in the short week she'd spent with him. As far as he was concerned, this was a purely physical relationship, and she knew it was important she maintain the same attitude… or at least the illusion of that same attitude.

"Fine, I get that. I know I've been known to announce my love and devotion to a guy only to have him dump me the next week."

"Look, all I'll say is that it's been really exciting these past days; exhausting, but a thrill a minute. The sex is amazing and everything in between is great. We spend much of every day together and there hasn't been one moment I wasn't happy to be with him. He's a great cook and he spoils me like you wouldn't believe. It's almost embarrassing."

"I'm happy for you sweetie. You deserve someone who'll spoil you. You've worked so hard this past year." Laura looked thoughtful as she sipped her wine. "Is he cute?"

"Huh?"

"This new guy… is he cute?"

"Yeah, really. I mean, no. He's beyond cute. He's gorgeous." She emptied her glass of wine and set it on the coffee table.

"When do you think you'll introduce me?" Not missing a step, Laura refilled Serena's glass.

"It's only been a couple of weeks, Laura. Give me a month or so." Eager to change the subject, Serena stood. "I'm going to go to the bathroom."

Laura leaned back and grinned. "You can't escape me now, Serena."

With a chuckle, Serena made her way to the bathroom. She knew Laura meant well. Maybe she should just come out and tell her about Sebastian; perhaps not the entire truth about their living arrangement, but at least that he was the one she was involved with these days.

She closed the bathroom door behind her, but before she could even unzip her jeans, she spotted Laura's latest bathroom reading material and her heart sank. Grabbing the magazine, she ran back to the living room. "What is this?"

Stunned, Laura turned to look at her. "It's a magazine, Serena. My God, have you been cooped up that long?"

"No! This!" She slapped the page that'd been left open for all to see. "What's this?"

"Oh, that. Yeah, it's your professor. I wanted to show you that. Your professor is quite the catch."

Serena sank back into her seat and stared at the photo of Sebastian. Handsome in a dark blue stylish suit, he stood beside Willow. With his arm loosely wrapped around her waist, he looked directly into the camera, a wistful smile on his lips. Willow, for her part, was beaming.

"Did you know he was planning on getting married?" Laura said with utter innocence.

"No," Serena growled as she tossed the magazine on the sofa.

"Gee, Serena. What's with you? I know he's your professor, but what's the big deal?" Laura picked up the magazine. "I think it's a pretty nice picture. This Willow girl is really pretty. She seems nice."

"Nice? Are you crazy, Laura? She's a gold-digger."

"I don't get it. You're usually so..." She stopped and stared at Serena. "Oh, my God. He's... Is he...? Serena... your professor? Are you banging...?"

The Protégé by Kailin Gow

Closing her eyes, Serena leaned back and let out an exhausted sigh.

Chapter 15

As he walked back to his rental car, Sebastian envisioned his next encounter with Serena. It'd been a week since he'd seen her and he missed her; her body, her touch, her kisses. He craved her in a way that was completely foreign to him. Accustomed to being in control of his senses, of having the upper hand when it came to relationships, he now felt strangely under her control, though he felt certain she was unaware of the control she had over him.

The sound of the moans and groans that accompanied her orgasms rang in his ear. Serena didn't have the habitual, typical, porn movie sighs and cries that so many women tried to fake. Her moans came from deep within. The sound was rooted in something so feral, so ancient, it never failed to arouse him. It was the part of her she kept hidden to the world, yet with him, she was alive, passionate, a woman with deep needs he aimed to fulfill.

With a quiet groan of his own, he adjusted the uncomfortable tightness that now filled his pants and tried to think of something else.

He didn't have to think too hard. On turning the corner he saw the car he'd rented for his stay in Seattle. Even from a distance he noticed the odd angle of the car and knew he had a flat tire. Cursing his bad luck, approached the car and realized the tire wasn't flat; it'd been slashed.

Adding to the fear and fury of knowing someone could deliberately slash not one, but two tires, was the photo pinned under the windshield wiper. It was the same picture that had appeared in the society pages; the photo of him with his arm around Serena, only Serena's face was scratched out; violently scratched out.

He felt sick to his stomach and leaned against the car as he tried to make sense of it all. His suspicions immediately went to Willow, but he quickly dismissed that notion. Though she was eager to marry him, he couldn't imagine she'd go to such lengths.

Quickly running through former lovers, he tried to determine who could do such a thing. None of them had been particularly jealous or possessive. They'd known he was in it for the fun and play, and that a serious relationship was out of the question.

He turned to look at the car again. Whoever had done this wasn't happy about his relationship with Serena, and if they'd done this to him here, now, what could they have done back home to Serena?

Chapter 16

The first flight back to Irvine had Sebastian in his apartment by nine o'clock the next morning. Eager to see her and hold her in his arms, to assess for himself that she was okay, he ran through the apartment, calling her name.

After a few minutes of yelling like a madman, he finally had to accept the obvious. Serena wasn't home. Despite his warnings she not leave the security of his building, she'd gone out. When he called her cell phone, she didn't answer, adding to the growing sense of dread that'd been building up.

Perhaps she'd just gone down for the mail. Perhaps she'd decided to go to the cleaners.

No, he finally decided. He wasn't going to wait around to see. Certain something had happened to her, he rushed out and headed to her apartment.

Once there he banged on her door and was confronted by a beautiful, but clearly angry woman.

"Well, well. If it isn't Professor love 'em and leave 'em hanging."

"What?" he said with exasperation. "Who are you? Where's Serena?"

Leaving the door open behind her, Laura returned to the boxes and suitcases she'd been packing. "I'm Laura, Serena's best friend."

"What are you doing?"

Laura looked at him, her gaze scrutinizing, assessing and accusatory all at the same time. "I can see why Serena is so taken with you. You are a looker... but that wasn't enough to keep her pining over you."

"What the hell are you talking about? I was out of town for a week. I left her a note. I even called her at the beginning of the week. She knew where I was. She knew I was coming back."

"Yeah, right." Unimpressed, Laura opened Serena's top dresser drawer and threw a few personals into a suitcase.

"Look, you don't know the whole story. Serena knew she could be in danger if she left my apartment. I took great care to ensure her safety, but I could only do that as long as she stayed put."

"I know more about this story than you think."

Sebastian looked at her and gestured with his hand for her to go on.

"Serena has been getting some warning signals these past few days."

Cocking his head to the side, he kept his eyes steadily on her, though he felt his gut fill with dread.

"At first it was phone calls; someone asking strange questions about her; who she was, where she was from, what she was doing." Laura sat on the bed, her hands filled with socks. "When she stopped answering her phone, they left messages. They quickly became more and more obscene, asking what size cup she wore, how often she had sex, how naughty she was… things like that."

"Like a stalker?"

"Exactly. After a few days she simply turned off her phone."

"That's why I couldn't reach her after that first phone call," Sebastian muttered.

"Anyway, that's her business." Laura stood, tossed the socks in the suitcase, and began throwing books and magazines into a box. "She's not your concern anymore."

"Why wouldn't I be concerned with her?" Stunned, Sebastian tried to make sense of what this stranger was telling him.

"I would think Willow Brookes was enough to keep you busy these days, what with picking out china patterns and all that crap."

Sebastian snorted. "What does Willow have to do with this?"

Laura shot him a menacing glare. "Look here, Mr. Professor. Just because you're a hottie doesn't mean you can string Serena along, have sex with her on the side, while planning your grand wedding to that socialite bitch."

"Wedding? Are you nuts?"

"No, sir. The one who's nuts is you. I'm only thankful Serena learned about the true nature of her relationship with you now rather than later. I mean, just how long were you planning on stringing her along, anyway?"

"Look, first off, I wasn't stringing her along. I'm not stringing her along. I don't know where the hell you got this idea about a wedding, but Serena knows damn well how I feel about Willow. What insane ideas have you been putting in her head?"

211

Laura straightened up and looked him in the eye. "I didn't have to put anything in her head. She saw it for herself, in black and white. You and Willow make an adorable couple, at least that's how it seemed in the romantic picture they had of you guys in the society pages."

Sebastian sat on the bed and stared dumbfounded at the box Laura had been packing.

"As if that wasn't bad enough, when Serena went back to your place to get her things, there was a message on your voicemail. She thought it might be you, so she checked. It was your mother. She was thrilled with the news of your impending marriage and was looking forward to helping Willow with the arrangements. She congratulated you for finally coming to your senses." Laura leaned back against the wall. Her voice dropped to a soft mutter as she continued, "She was happy you'd finally grown up and you'd put an end to dating such inconsequential girls."

"My God," Sebastian whispered. "Serena heard all that?"

"You bet."

"But she knows how my mother can be. She knows how my mother feels about Willow."

"All I can say is I was there to pick up the pieces, and it wasn't pretty."

"So, where is she now?"

Laura crossed her arms before her and a guarded shadow veiled her eyes.

"I need to know where she is. I have to talk to her, to make her understand what's going on."

Laura remained silent, but Sebastian could see she was debating whether to talk or not. Wanting to remain patient, he didn't push for an answer and simply hoped this woman would see he had Serena's best interest at heart.

"I know she's safe," she finally said. "Though I don't believe she's in the healthiest of positions."

"What does that mean?"

Again, Sebastian had to wait through a long and tense silence. "Damn it, where is she?" Sebastian growled. "I'll find out one way or another."

Laura pressed her lips together then looked at him, her gaze defeated and tired. "She's with him."

A strange and painful sting gripped his heart. "What do you mean? A boyfriend? Her ex?" The words choked him.

Letting out a sardonic chuckle, Laura blurted out, "Ha, he's never been much of a boyfriend to her; the way he treated her."

"Then what?"

"Her master." The moment she's spoken the word, Laura brought her hand over her mouth in disbelief. "I was never supposed to tell you that, but… My God, I know it's not good for her to be with him. She's left him years ago to break the bond and go off on her own, pursue her dreams of a music career, live a normal life…"

Sebastian's eyes looked stricken. "What do you mean? Is Serena in some kind of trouble?"

Laura cringed. "I've said too much already."

Chapter 17

"Serena, what are you doing out in the cold?"

Standing on the penthouse balcony that offered a magnificent view of the ocean that gleamed under the moonlight, Serena didn't respond to the gentle but firm voice that called to her. Yes, the night air was chilled and she stood wearing only a flimsy white silk gown and silk panties, but the cold was the last thing on her mind.

Her taste of freedom had been brief; too brief. She'd experienced life in a way that was foreign to her, but she'd quickly come to savor every part of that experience. Though she'd initially feared what awaited her outside his protective circle, what would happen were she not bonded to him, were she not at his side, she'd quickly surmounted that fear.

Waves crashed far below, reminding her of the wild child that still resided inside her; the wild child that wanted to venture far and wide, to go where she choose, unbridled, uninhibited; to take chances, no matter the risk.

Was she truly prepared to return inside the safety of the cage she'd known? Did she really want to leave behind the world she'd come to know? This past year she'd made friends, notably Laura, whom she cherished. She'd gotten her feet wet in an ocean of music and had truly had every intention of pursuing a career in composition. But most of all, she'd found someone who surprised her; someone who brought out in her everything she'd always wanted to be.

Yes, Sebastian could be difficult at times. He was demanding and his hands could be rough while making love to her, but that passion... At the thought of his lips, his tongue, his hands, heat swelled inside her and left a thin layer of moisture over her chilled limbs.

Shaking her head, she shoved those heated thoughts aside. As amusing as those passionate nights had been, she had to accept the fact that she was a mere plaything where he was concerned. While she'd captured him in her bed, Willow was the one who'd captured the rest of him.

She bit back the tears of frustration. She missed him already and knew he'd be in her heart longer than she'd expected. That had been the mistake; allowing her heart to warm to him. Though their time together had been relatively short, she'd quickly felt the strong stirrings of emotion for him. It was the one rule she shouldn't have crossed…getting emotionally involved with the target. Especially in her role playing.

But things have gotten complicated, not at all what she had anticipated. Him getting poisoned, the apartment being ransacked, and then the attack on her. Someone else had entered the party…someone she and her protégé Olivia, didn't anticipate. Plus the whole thing with Willow and the Sorensens…

Warm, strong hands encircled her waist and the hard caress of her Master's need pressed into her backside, erasing all thoughts of Sebastian. His greedy fingers found the slit in her gown and quickly slipped under her silk panties, knowing exactly where to touch to bring her to immediate climax. They dipped inside, finding heat and moisture while his other hand plucked at one breast then the other until they were both hard and attentive.

As much as Serena loved Sebastian, she couldn't deny the affection she had for this man, her Master. She owed him so much and without him, she couldn't even imagine where she'd be; what she'd be.

Probably still on the streets where he'd found her when she was only nineteen; probably begging, stealing, or worse. She would have never known the luxury of his magnificent suite and all of the spoils that came with his incredible wealth. She would have never tasted the exquisite joys of making love. He'd been her first, and he'd taken great care to teach her the intricacies of pleasure. He'd taken great pride in molding her into his ideal sexual creature, though taking care to keep her looking pure and innocent while she'd become a creature all men desired. And capable of taking on many sexual roles like a seasoned actress.

"How does this feel, Serena?" he murmured into her ear. He licked her lobe, pulled it between his teeth and sucked. When she remained silent, he turned her to face him. With increased determination, his fingers plunged in deeper, seeking the special spot that always pleased her. "What has you so silent, my beloved? Cat got your tongue?"

Her lips parted and her lids fell heavily over her eyes, but the moans he awaited failed to come.

"I'll remedy that fast enough," he whispered, his voice deep, husky and commanding. His fingers worked in perfect harmony, one reaching deep inside her while two more played with the folds of moist skin. His free hand slipped the strap off her shoulder, baring her breast. With hunger that bordered on savage, he clasped his lips to her nipple and sucked for a brief moment before pulling back to look at her. "I'll ask you again. How does that feel?"

"Good."

"Good, what?" He reached around to soundly smack her bottom.

A shiver of pleasure and pain shot through her. "Good, Master."

"What if I stopped?"

"No. Don't stop." These were the sensations that always left her weak; that always left her begging for more. The pleasure he brought her was intoxicating and impossible to resist, and her Master knew it all too well. He knew how to play her; how to tease her and how to drive her to the brink of insanity, all with his touch.

"What do you want me to do?"

She wanted to be strong enough to tell him to wait. She knew it was what he truly had in mind; to torture her with anticipation. "I want you inside me," she finally said. "I want you to fill me, to stroke me, to fuck me until I can't walk straight for weeks."

He chuckled, a pleased sound that resonated from deep in his chest. In one quick motion, he pulled his fingers out of her and jacked her up onto the cement railing that encircled the balcony. His hard fingers pried her knees apart and he stared at her.

She should have been afraid. So high above the beach, the street, the people who went about their business far below, she would normally have been more concerned with her safety than anything else. But now that danger seemed insignificant. It was the void left by his fingers that was unbearable. It was the need to be touched by him that took precedence.

"I'm not ready to plunge into you just yet." He sneered while his gaze swept over her.

"Then your mouth."

"What would you have me do with my mouth?"

"Taste me. Warm me with your mouth. Make love to me with your tongue and lips."

He wrapped his arms around her waist and leaned over to slide his tongue under her panties. The moment his tongue reached the sensitive nub of skin

220

that beckoned his touch, she quivered with joy and clung to him. Her fingers dug into his neck while her legs wrapped around his waist.

"I want you inside me," she commanded. "Oh, God, how I want you inside me. I want to feel you pounding against me. I need…" *to forget Sebastian Sorensen.*

"Missed me?" Her Master said. It wasn't a question, but a statement.

"Yes," she breathed, writhing against his skillful tongue. "Oh, please fill me now, Master."

"Do you regret leaving me, leaving this, leaving everything?" He paused his thorough licking for a moment to run a finger down her breast, her stomach, and into her hard.

Serena shuddered with need and pleasure. "Yes, Master. I did."

He leaned in and whispered into her ears, "I gave you everything I had. Everything I own, but it wasn't enough."

"I love you for it, but it wasn't enough," Serena said. "I needed a life of my own, to follow my own dreams, not be your shadow, your submissive forever."

"But you were born to be, Serena. We were made for each other." He increased the pressure and the rhythm of his fingers, causing her to moan and cry out.

"Oh, fuck it. I was wrong. I belong with you, and you need to get your dick into me now…Master."

He chuckled. "The old Serena, the hot-tempered, impatient Serena from the streets is talking, isn't she?"

"Yes, and right now, she wants a good banging up the wall, right here, while stark naked on our balcony facing the ocean. I want you to now, dammit."

"Not yet." He brought his tongue back to the furthest reaches of her moistened lips and gave her a few slow, tantalizing licks.

The pleasure left her dizzy and giddy.

With a throaty moan that displayed his arousal, he picked her up and brought her inside. Her fingers dug through his thick waves of golden hair as her lips taunted the warm skin of his neck, causing him to groan.

As he'd done so many times before, he set her on his bed and reached for the silken straps that'd been sewn into the four corners of the bed. With unhurried patience, he bound one wrist, then worked at binding her other wrist, though with more urgency. When he bound her ankles, he was clearly impatient, tying her so tightly, she knew she'd have marks to show for it the next day.

"Now?" she asked.

He reached for one of her favorite silk ties; the pale green one that matched his eyes.

"I'd like to be able to see you, Master."

"Not this time." He covered her eyes with the tie and knotted it behind her head. "Such beautiful eyes, Serena. Men could drown in them. Make them weak with need for you."

"Now?" she asked again.

"Now, what?"

"Now, Master."

"Who do you belong to?" he asked. "Who have you always belonged to?"

"You," Serena replied. "I've always belonged to you." She groaned in anticipation as she heard the sound of wrapping paper being opened and the subtle sound of latex unraveling.

A few seconds later, she felt his weight on the bed, then felt the heat of his skin against hers. His lips played over her skin, teasing, tickling and arousing. "It's been so long since I've kissed you all over like this, Serena. I want to savor it. I want to make you mine all over again. I want to make you forget anyone and everyone who has ever come between us. Inch by tantalizing inch."

Unable to wait any longer, Serena lifted her hips up toward him. "Now, Master. Please relieve this hunger now."

Straightening his arms, he held himself off her a long moment, his breath hot and heavy as he silently tortured her. He glided his hardness through the moisture that awaited him then plunged deep inside her. "Like this!"

Serena let out a feral growl as his ample hard penis filled her completely, plunging deeper and deeper, arching his flexible muscular back. His lips caressed her breasts, heightening the pleasure he brought her. Though she wanted to extend the pleasure, to feel his skin against hers last all night, her body was ready to explode within minutes.

With an orgasmic cry that filled the room, her body shook, her hips rising up to meet his as he, too, let out an animalistic howl.

"My Serena. My beautiful girl, so beautiful, so innocent, so perfectly wild right where I need you to be." Releasing the ties at her wrists, he lay beside her. As he held her, he stroked her hair and kissed her temple.

She'd forgotten how gentle he could be. More often than not, he'd proven to be rough in his love making and harsh in his demands. He was her Master, and that was his right. But, occasionally, his hand was soft and loving.

For all his gentle caresses, she knew she'd have more than one marking to remind her of this night. Playful bites on her shoulder would mark her for days as would the bruising from the hard fingers that squeezed too tightly on her thighs.

Camouflaging those marks had become second nature to her.

"Master," she said with great reverence. "When will it be my turn?"

"When you make the switch?"

"I have already," she said. "Months after leaving you, I made the switch."

"But when it comes to me, Serena, what am I to you?"

225

"My Master," she said. "My Master, my love, my everything."

"And I am yours," he said, kissing her.

Chapter 18

Sebastian realized the extent of danger he'd put Serena in, but getting Laura to understand that danger was proving difficult. She remained tight-lipped about Serena's whereabouts.

"Okay," he finally said. "Stay right there and I'll be back in a minute."

Reprimanding himself for not thinking of it sooner, he rushed down to his car. In the trunk he found his suitcase, unzipped a compartment and pulled out the picture of Serena. Certain this would convince Laura of the danger that surrounded Serena, he hurried back up to her apartment.

"Look at what I found on the windshield of my car." He shoved the photo in her hand. "That was all the way in Seattle."

Laura visibly blanched.

"Now do you believe me?"

"Okay, so someone isn't too happy to see you with Serena," she said after a long moment of contemplation. "That being said, I'm sure she's safe where she is, at least with regards to whoever scratched her face out like this." She held up the photo. "Her master has always taken care of her."

Sebastian cringed, white hot jealousy shot through him like he's never felt before. As far as he was concerned, Serena was his now.

"Besides, that still doesn't change the fact that you played with her while planning to marry another."

"I told you. I have no intention of marrying another. For the time being, I have no intention of marrying anyone." A sense of desperation took over him. Time was ticking away and he was losing patience. "Look, I cut my business trip short because I felt it was important to come and protect Serena. Are you really willing to let her remain in danger? This Master you talk about, if he doesn't know the danger Serena is in, he might not be in a position to really help her."

Laura stared at him, her lips parted with the desire to answer him.

"I flew back from Seattle just to see her. I care that much about her. I'd do anything to protect her... and I'll do anything to get her back. She's all I think about. Not an hour goes by when I can't wait to get back to her, to be with her." Sebastian shook his head.

He'd never admit it, but Serena had now become part of his reason for breathing. She was everything to him.

"Anything?"

"Anything and everything."

"Then, my dear Professor, you'd better be prepared for just that… everything, because that is the price he'll want for her. Don't expect him to just stand aside and let you take over. He'll make you move heaven and earth before he'll relinquish his power over her."

Turning away, Sebastian snorted in frustration. "My God. What has she gotten herself into? How in the world did she get mixed up in something so crazy?"

"The woman you met is quite different from the young woman she was a few years ago."

Sebastian turned back to her.

"It might not look like it now, but she had a rough start. Her parents weren't around and she had to pretty much raise herself. She'd been out on the streets for over six months when he found her. She was a skeleton of the girl you know, but somehow he saw something beautiful in her. From what she's told me, he changed her life. He saved her life. He taught her what life could be, if she trusted him. He fed her, clothed her and pampered her. He also turned her into the lover he desired."

His skin went cold as he thought of his nights with Serena. How the thought of another man touching her, brought murderous rage in him. No one can touch her like he can…break through that innocence to see the wild woman she was underneath. Yes, he'd noticed just how talented she was. He'd enjoyed every physical contact he'd had with her. Her touch was comparable to that of an expert, but he'd simply thought she had that natural instinct. He'd never even allowed for the possibility of her prior experience with such a man as this master Laura spoke of.

"On more than one occasion she's told me just how indebted she is towards him. She feels she owes him everything, including herself."

"That's ridiculous. In this day and age? In this country? How can anyone belong to another?"

"I guess unless you've been through what she's been through, you can't really understand. Believe me, I did try to help her adjust to life outside his realm. I tried to help her live a normal life. In the past little while she'd become stronger. She was determined to rebuild her life, her way. Regaining her self-esteem and confidence was difficult, but she was getting there."

"Her love of music..." Sebastian muttered as he stared off into space. In his mind's eye, he saw her, so innocent, so naïve, so willing and eager to learn.

"Yes. I think music played a big part in saving her. She clung to it like a buoy and put her heart and soul into it."

"Yeah. I'll admit she's been a very determined student."

"Unfortunately, the spell he has over her is stronger than her love of music."

"I find that hard to believe."

"That's the hold he has on her. He controls her like a marionette. Looks like he did a great job of training her. She'll do whatever he asks of her."

"It seems so unlike her."

"She does hold great affection for him."

"You think she loves him?" Sebastian asked incredulously.

"It might not be a healthy love, but, yes, I do think she loves him."

Never a man to hold an ounce of jealousy, Sebastian wanted to fall back from the force of the painful impact. The thought of Serena with him; with this man, any man other than himself... it twisted his gut in a way that bordered on excruciating.

When he looked at Laura, he saw sympathy in her eyes.

"You really care about her, huh?" she asked.

"Yeah, I..." He choked and coughed, surprised by the intensity of emotion he felt. "I do."

Laura nodded.

"Where is she?" His question was soft spoken, almost defeated.

"She'll kill me for this, but..." Laura walked to the kitchen and found her purse. She pulled out a little pink notebook with a matching pen attached to it with a small pink elastic band. After shooting one last skeptical glance at Sebastian, she scribbled on the first page of the notebook and ripped the sheet out. "Here."

He reached out for the sheet of paper, but she quickly withdrew it.

"This is where she's staying. I'd like nothing better than to have you succeed in getting her back; in getting her out of there. At least with you, you can help her live a normal life – one which she'll be able to be the master or mistress of her own life. I owe Serena a lot. She put up with a lot of shit from me when I hit a few rough patches a while back. I hope she'd consider this payback. I hope she'll realize that I'm doing this for her own good.

"I'm sure she will." Once again, he reached for the sheet of paper, but she held it aloft.

"I hope you'll help her move forward and not allow her to fall deeper into the black hole that will surely swallow her up for good this time."

"I'll do my best."

"But, if you break her heart, if you get her away from her master only to turn around and break her heart, you will have me to contend with." She glared at him. "You understand me?"

"Perfectly."

She handed him the address and he hurried out. He'd already lost far too much time and didn't want to waste another minute.

Mindful of the traffic that surrounded him, he drove as quickly as he could to the building that was familiar to him. He knew many of the people who lived in the prestigious building and had a gnawing suspicion who occupied the penthouse. As he rode the elevator to the top floor, he prayed he was wrong.

Chapter 19

The door opened before he had the chance to knock and he faced the suspicions that'd grown on the way up.

"Price," Sebastian said with a cool nod. It was in sharp contrast to the blood that boiled so feverishly under his skin.

Wearing only black silk pants, the handsome blond stood in the doorway, confident in all that he was.

Sebastian's jaw tightened as he accepted the fact that this man, this master of Serena, was a very good looking man. He obviously worked hard at staying in shape and for a flashing moment, Sebastian imagined this man over Serena's body.

He wanted to vomit.

"Mr. Sorensen," Price said. "What brings you here?"

Sebastian's fingers twitched as he fought the urge to reach out and grab the young tycoon by the throat.

"I thought I'd settled everything with your father." Price leaned his toned torso into the door frame and crossed his arms over his chest, emphasizing the strength of his muscles.

Yes, Sebastian thought. And his father wouldn't be too thrilled when he learned of this latest revelation.

Cocking a brow, Price grinned. "You seem kind of lost. Are you sure you're at the right place?"

Sebastian could have sworn the arrogant bastard flexed his biceps.

"I got this address for Serena Singleton." Holding his breath, he hoped and prayed he had the wrong address. Perhaps Laura had given him the wrong address. It could have even been an intentional mistake… anything to get rid of him, to throw him off Serena's track.

"Yeah, what do you want with her?"

His heart ceased beating for an aching moment. Serena was here… with this man… with this damned arrogant man who clearly didn't deserve her.

"Who is that?" An authoritative female voice called out.

Sebastian's heart resumed beating, but at a frantic pace. It was Serena's voice, but with a tone he'd never heard before. Gone was the innocent student voice that was so soft, feminine, and pleasing.

Dressed in a skimpy white silk teddy, her hair tousled and wild, Serena came to stand beside Price. She casually leaned into him, as though they'd been lovers for ages. Sebastian could only stare, taking in her scent, her smooth skin, the hair he had wrapped around his fingers many times before. God, she was sexy, and every part of him wanted to go over, grab her, and make love to her right now.

Lazily, almost indifferently, she looked to Sebastian. After a shocked moment of gaping, she smiled at him, a smile that betrayed nothing of the relationship they'd had, nothing of the passionate nights they'd shared; nothing of nothing. Judging by her polite but detached smile, they were mere acquaintances; or worse still, they'd never met.

The moment Laura had given him the address, he'd had every intention of tearing Serena out of the grips of this master, of freeing her, but now… he felt an immense loss. The animal instinct that had driven him to this man's penthouse now faded to nothing.

Though he ached, he had no idea how to deal with the woman that now faced him; this woman he'd come to care so much for. Her indifference to him, floored him.

She seemed so content and at ease with this pompous blond man. She seemed completely at home in the luxury penthouse. Laura had spoken of this master as though he were Serena's captor, her slave driver, but Serena seemed far from being imprisoned or enslaved. When she looked up at her master, her eyes warm with admiration and affection, a part of Sebastian crumbled inside.

"It looks like we have a visitor, Serena," Price said. He seemed unperturbed by Serena's lack of adequate clothing, just as Serena seemed perfectly at home parading around in a teddy that left nothing to the imagination. Despite himself, Sebastian grew hard just looking at her, remembering what it felt like to touch her and taste her every night and morning.

She nodded and took Sebastian's hand, not as a lover or friend, but as a hostess intent on welcoming a guest. Leading him into the living room, she said, "Could I bring you a glass of wine? Or perhaps you'd prefer coffee?"

"I'm good, thanks." Sebastian sat on the black leather sofa and watched Serena as she stood at Price's side as he took a seat.

"This young man is here to see you, Serena. Do you wonder why?"

"I do."

Sebastian gazed at Serena then at Price. Was he expected to state his reason for coming to see Serena right there in front of this arrogant bastard? He would have preferred to talk to her alone, to have the chance to reach out to her, to hold her hand, to... He took a deep breath and accepted the situation as it presented itself. Price's possessive glare clearly told him that a private reunion with Serena would not happen.

"First off," Sebastian finally said. He held Serena's gaze, hoping to convey the emotion that accompanied his words. "I wanted to clear up all this Willow marriage business. The society pages picked up on that picture of me with Willow and they ran with it, no doubt encouraged by Willow herself and her mother. I have no intention whatsoever of marrying that woman. She knows it, her mother knows it and my mother knows it. That article was all wishful thinking on their part." For a moment he forgot about Price's presence as he looked into Serena's eyes. "You know me better than that, Serena. For crying out loud, if I'd wanted to marry her, I'd be with her now, not here trying to get you back."

"Get her back?" Price said with a menacing tone.

Ignoring him, Sebastian kept his eyes on Serena. "I want to go back to the way we were before…"

Price whipped his head back to look at Serena. "Is that what you'd want? To go back to the way you were? The way you were with him?"

Sebastian held her gaze. Her eyes had softened at his question, but had become defensive when Price had questioned her. If they could have a moment alone, Sebastian felt certain she'd come to him; that she'd give him a second chance.

"Serena," Sebastian murmured. "Please give us another chance."

"I think I would like that."

"Like what?" Price shot out.

"I would like to start again. I would like to go back to the way it was." Though there was affection and warmth in her eyes, something was missing.

Sebastian felt a ball of pain and regret take hold in his gut. Something was holding her back and he didn't know if he'd be able to get her past it.

"But…" Price interjected.

Serena cast her gaze to Price's shoulder.

"There are a few things Sebastian needs to know about you. I wouldn't want him to have the false impression that he has the capacity to make you happy; to keep you happy, right Serena?"

She nodded but kept her gaze fixed to Price's shoulder.

"Serena?" Sebastian said, hoping to snap her out of the hold this man had on her.

Chapter 20

From below her lashes, Serena looked at Sebastian. From the very first time she'd met him, she'd been aware of the difference between him and Price. She'd even wondered if that had been part of the appeal. Visually, he was dark and brooding where Price was fair and outgoing. Internally, however, the two men seemed to switch extremities, leaving Price with the dark and sometimes foreboding demeanor, while Sebastian proved how sweet and kind he could be.

Now, as she gazed at him, she felt the strong stirrings she'd felt for him right from the start. Though she wanted to cling to the hurt and anger that had accosted her when she'd found out about his wedding to Willow, deep inside, she believed him. She believed he truly wanted to be with her… to win her back.

His strength and determination faltered as he waited for her to respond to him. He suddenly seemed so beaten down; so defeated, and she knew she was responsible for that pained look in his eyes. As much

242

as she would have liked to change that, there was little she could do about it now. Their paths had crossed. Their paths had mingled. And now their paths must diverge.

And so life went on.

"Serena?" Sebastian said again, the pleading tone of his voice enough to make her weep. "Do you believe I don't have what you need to make you happy? Do you not believe that I would do everything and anything to make you happy?"

Flashes of her nights with Price came to her; nights that were torrid, heated and satisfying. Sometimes their play turned rough. While she never would admit it to anyone, she enjoyed those nights. The pain Price inflicted on her brought out something animal and instinctual in her, something she never failed to respond to. She couldn't deny Price had the magic touch, and while Sebastian had proven to have the potential to please her just as much, she didn't know yet how far he'd go. Now, she wished she'd tested him more when she'd had the chance. She wished she'd pressed him to go outside his comfort zone.

But more than anything, she simply wished she'd had the chance to tell him what Price now wanted to expose of her. She knew how he played. He wanted to strip away the image of the innocent girl she played. He wanted to show Sebastian what he was truly up against. He wanted Sebastian to see the dark and wild animal that resided in her.

No doubt he felt Sebastian wouldn't be up to the task of pleasing her. She could already hear the victorious tone in his voice.

He slapped her bottom and looked up at her. "I think Sebastian Sorensen, the noted professor and prized composer, would like to know more about you Serena Singleton. I highly doubt he'll be pleased with what you have to show him of yourself, but I think watching him squirm as he discovers you, could be amusing. There's something fascinating in watching a pious, highly noted and accomplished professional crumble in the face of black leather, strap-ons and sex swings. It's always a pleasure to watch a man's eyes darken with confusion, then widen with arousal as he learns that the innocent woman he'd come to care so much for is not so innocent at all."

Sebastian's eyes darkened and hardened. He'd not seen anything yet, and clearly he wasn't pleased. When Price slipped his fingers under the frail fabric of her panties and grabbed her bottom, Sebastian gripped the armrests and Serena was certain he'd lunge at him, but he remained immobile.

"I'm anxious to see if you'll be aroused, Professor Sorensen."

Sebastian grimaced and chewed on his inner cheek.

"Nice ass, wouldn't you say?" Price taunted as he kneaded Serena's firm but round butt cheek.

Sebastian's gaze jumped from the workings of Price's hand to Serena's eyes. How could she let this arrogant ass, show her off like this? The Serena he knew, who stood up to his parents at the fundraiser, wouldn't allow her bottom to be handled like that in front of people. His eyes pleaded, begged and sought to understand. Was Laura right? Did Serena's return to her Master squelched her spirit as a person, too? Where was the Serena he knew?

Chapter 21

Having spent a good portion of the night weeping after seeing how hurt Sebastian looked when Serena acted like she never knew him, never cared for him, Serena got out of bed the moment she heard Price leave the penthouse. The night with him had been heated and they'd had little chance to sleep. If their little spectacle last night didn't arouse Sebastian, it had certainly turned Price on. He'd been insatiable, coming back again and again, and wanting more and more. His requests had gone beyond anything he'd ever asked of her before, leaving her sore and sensitive all over.

By the time he awoke late that morning and left to go to the office, she'd been awake for hours. Her mind had played and replayed the events of the night before, trying to make sense of everything that had happened. She'd wept in silence as Price had slept soundly. She'd been desperate to keep him from knowing just how heartbroken she was about

246

Sebastian. He'd only ridicule and torment her about her failure to keep her emotions in check.

Her bare feet were soothed by the warm thick carpeting of his bedroom as she stepped to the window and pulled back the heavy drapes. For a brief moment she was blinded by the brilliant sun. It was a shame. Her mood would have preferred a gray and rainy day.

As far as the eye could see, sunlight glistened on every tiny wavelet of the peaceful ocean. Occasionally the sun hit on the sail of an elegant sailboat. Far below, people strolled or jogged on the beach sand while others milled around the dock as they prepared for a leisurely boat ride, or an afternoon of fishing.

From the outside, it promised to be a beautiful day; the type of day Serena usually hoped for; the type of day that left a spring in her step; the type of day that made her smile for no other reason than the sun on her face and the breeze in her hair. Yet today, the day seemed doomed to be dark and painful. No amount of sunshine or laughter would alleviate that.

Still strapped into the leather corset she'd put on the night before, she headed to the kitchen to get a cup of coffee. As she passed the hall mirror she caught a glimpse of herself and immediately thought of Sebastian.

In her mind's eye, she saw his eyes as Price had exposed her true nature. Shock had mingled with arousal. He'd been intrigued, but had held back. His gaze had held restrained interest. His eyes had widened one moment and he'd even protested a time or two, but the slow lick of his lips and the subtle narrowing of his eyes had betrayed him.

"Go get dressed," Price had ordered. "Sebastian and I are going to enjoy a moment of male bonding."

She'd not heard their exchange as she'd left the room to dun the clothing Price requested, but she'd noticed the red splotches on Sebastian's face when she'd returned. What exploits had Price regaled him with? During her brief absence, she'd heard Price's throaty laugh, the type of laugh he usually reserved for the people he didn't particularly like; for the people he was happy to hurt. She knew Price can be cruel like that when he was set on winning. Being one of the youngest self-made billionaires, he knew how to be ruthless.

As she'd exited the room she shared with her master, her steps had been tentative at first. Destroying the image she'd created for Sebastian was at once painful and thrilling. How would he react? What would he say? Aroused by the very notion, she walked out and hoped he'd be ready to get in the game. She longed for nothing more than to show him her true colors and to have him appreciate all those colors.

When she turned the corner and entered the living room, Sebastian's jaw dropped and he instantly stopped talking. His disbelieving gaze took in the tight red corset that left her breasts almost completely exposed. Her nipples were erect and her breasts hard with want of a strong hand. His gaze dipped to the thigh high, four inch heeled boots, and the riding crop.

"You sure you want her?" Price had taunted.

Sebastian didn't say anything, but from the heated look in his burning blue eyes, it was clear he wanted her.

Serena shook the images from her head and tried to shake off the intense arousal her reverie had brought. She'd wanted so badly to play with Sebastian; to show him what she could do to him; what she could make him do to her. In the end, she had to assume the shock of it all had been too much. Without saying a word, and without taking another look at her, he had gotten out of his seat so fast, Serena had frozen in place, speechless.

He'd left without saying a word and now she had no idea what he thought of what he'd seen. What, if anything, did he want of her.

With her cup of coffee in hand, she returned to the bedroom to find more suitable clothing for the day. After a night in the tight corset, she wanted to spend the rest of the morning in something loose and comfortable. Price would be gone for a good portion of the day and she wanted to go back to the innocent college girl for a little while. In a way, she was very much this girl who had wide-eyed innocence and dreams of a future in music. She sighed as a single teardrop fell on her cheek. It was worse, knowing how Sebastian had encouraged her all the way as a true professor and mentor. He truly thought she was talented, and understood how notes can meld together to form melodies that moved people. She was going to miss Sebastian…

She reached for the second drawer of Price's dresser hoping to find a soft and comfy t-shirt. No such luck. All he had was an assortment of boxers, boxer briefs and special mini briefs for those special nights, she knew too well.

She opened the bottom drawer and rummaged beneath the many polo shirts all nicely folded and sorted by color. Instead of finding soft t-shirts, however, her hand came over a thick envelope. Never one to pry, she now felt an irresistible urge to find out more about Price. For all their time together, he'd always been so private, so secretive. He'd given her tidbits of information about himself, but he'd always doled out that information with great care.

What could be the harm in knowing a little bit more about him? she thought. The envelope was heavy and clamped closed with a thick paper clip.

Sitting on the bed, she pried the paper clip off and pulled the flap up. Her heart beat at a quickened pace and she suddenly had the foreboding sense she was about to learn something she might not be happy to learn. Her fingers reached inside and prepared to pull the thick stack of paper out, but she needed a moment to catch her breath first.

Ignorance is bliss, she thought. Yeah, she silently countered, and curiosity killed the cat.

251

"Okay," she scolded herself. "Get it over with."

She pulled out the stack of paper and was confronted by a picture of herself and Sebastian; the same photo that had been taken on the yacht the night of the party.

Her heart sank. Why did Price have such a photo? Where had he gotten it?

Don't blow this all out of proportion, she reminded herself. The photo had appeared in the society pages and it was easily conceivable that Price, deeply concerned for Serena, should have the photo in his possession.

As logical as all that seemed, Serena wasn't convinced of the innocence surrounding the envelope and her picture, but why?

And more importantly, how long had he known of her relationship with Sebastian? Sebastian had been adamant about keeping the relationship private, at least for the time being.

She thought back to the night of that party. So many people had filled the yacht, all impeccably dressed. With the men all in tuxedo, they'd easily blended in with one another. Had Price been there that night, he could have easily missed Serena's sweeping gaze.

Thinking back to that night, she remembered how she'd thought of him. She'd looked for him. At the time it'd been just an amusing game. She'd felt certain of the improbability, but now... It was exactly the type of party that drew him in.

But why would he now want to keep this photo? Though Price could be possessive at times, he'd never been the type of man to be jealous. After all, their relationship had always been an exclusively physical one; there was nothing to be jealous about.

His attitude toward Sebastian the night before, however, left her with more questions than answers.

"Where were you before I came here, Price?" she called aloud.

The day she'd learned of Sebastian's impending marriage to Willow, she'd called him. She'd needed his reassurance, his comfort... his bed. She'd needed to wash away the love and affection that she had grown for Sebastian. Price was the perfect remedy. When he hadn't answered his home phone, she'd called his mobile phone.

Surprised when he'd answered, he'd been vague about his whereabouts. All he'd said was that he was out of town.

"Out where?" Serena now question. "Did you go to Seattle, Price? Are you the reason Sebastian came back to Irvine so quickly?"

She thought of Sebastian's week in the hospital and his suspicions.

No, she instantly thought. Price had better things to do than to poison the man she'd had a date with. At the time their relationship had not even begun.

But the ransacking of Sebastian's apartment...

For the next fifteen minutes she debated the possibilities. What did she really know about Price?

The remaining contents of the envelope gave her a bit more insight. Price had signed a contract with Sebastian's father. She skimmed over the documents, astonished by the amount of money that had exchanged hands.

Once again, she questioned Price's motive. The contract had been signed soon after her initial date with Sebastian; after the week she'd spent tending to him at the hospital. Was it all connected? Was it all coincidental?

"What are you up to, Price?"

It was hard to believe her new love and her old master were so connected; so intertwined.

As she continued to flip through the pages, she came upon a check list.

Most of it consisted of business talk – takeovers, mergers, dividends and stocks. Toward the bottom of the last page, however, she got a glimpse of Price's intention.

Her complete name was written in big block letters, Sebastian's full name beside it. Where her name was highlighted in yellow, Sebastian's name was struck out with a thick red line. Below it was the name of the company Sebastian's father had spent so many years building.

It, too, was struck out with a thick red line.

In the margin, scribbled with a pencil was a notation; "The Sorensens, the Brooks, Serena Singleton." What did it all mean? Serena knew Price had business dealings with the Sorensens and the Brooks, but what did it have to do with her? Surely, he wasn't so obsessive and jealous that he would destroy anyone who got in the way of him and Serena? Knowing Price, he can be completely devoid of emotions, especially love, when dealing in business. Not wasting another minute, she picked up the phone and dialed Sebastian's number. If he had any doubts whatsoever about their relationship, she wanted to put them to rest right away. She'd already toyed unnecessarily with his emotions and now she had to completely cut the ties…to protect Sebastian, to protect the Sorensens. For all the love and gentleness Price had shown her as her lover and even as her master, she knew he was a powerful man who didn't like when his property is taken. And being a little than obsessed with her, she was and always will be his, despite how she had left him and tried to live a life as close to normal as she could.

She regretted the innocent virgin she'd portrayed to Sebastian. Regretted that she took the ruse so far with him. She couldn't resist giving the handsome sexy music composer a taste of his own medicine. It may seem like a trifle little thing to him, and he must have forgotten it, but she remembered all too well the first time she had met him. The lengths she went through to get a chance to audition for him…taking on the identity of Lily at the private men's club she found out he was going to be at…Little

White Lily, the sweet submissive/dom, the innocent, a type he seemed to be drawn to, and she was a master at portraying.

Used to performing sexual role plays with Price, Serena delved deep into her role as Lily, the innocent stage performer, the seductress, the angel. For weeks she had prepared for her role as one of the performers at the private club, ready to perform whatever sexual fantasy the prominent members of the club wanted. She was completely into her role, mind, body, and character when she walked on stage, beckoned for Sebastian Sorensen to come to her, and invited him to kiss her breast on stage when her ruse was found out, and she was almost thrown out of the club for pretending to be a performer there.

Sebastian Sorensen was in Las Vegas, producing one of his musicals, a new one with an edgy twist, and he was going to be visiting the nightclub with some friends. A big fan of his music, she wanted to meet him and audition for his musical, and the only way she thought she could meet him was at the club that night.

She had left Price almost a year when she met Sebastian as Lily at the club. It was disastrous, and although there was serious chemistry between them, as soon as she opened her mouth to sing, he said she was "rough" and needed further training in front of everyone. She was humiliated, not so much for dressing like Little White Lily with her breasts practically hanging out in front of other people, but for Sebastian to say her voice wasn't good enough for his musical. Needless to say, humiliated and ashamed, she stopped going to auditions and gave up on trying to be a singer.

Instead, she found her calling in composing music, channeling all the angry and hurt feelings she had towards Sebastian Sorensen into writing music and composing, eventually ending up in the Music Program at UC Irvine, where she found out Sebastian Sorensen was a professor. Still stinging from his rejection in the audition, it was the prime opportunity Serena thought to get back at his arrogant ass, but still be able to learn from his brilliance, although she thought he was an arrogant ass. She didn't think it would turn out so differently, and that she would end up falling hard for him, despite her love for Price. Sebastian was not the arrogant man she had thought he was in the beginning, but someone who was misunderstood, flawed with demons that she had just began to discover. Though that innocent child still resided deep within her, Sebastian had deserved the truth. Though it was too late to change that, she had the capacity to change whatever notions he still had in his head.

"Sebastian?" she said when he picked up.

"Serena," he said with relief and surprise. "I'm so happy you called."

"Sebastian." She kept her tone of voice solid and strong. This wasn't the time to fall apart. "You left so quickly last night. I just wanted to make sure everything was clear between us."

"I didn't leave because of what I learned about you. I don't care about all that, and I'm prepared to do anything you need to be happy."

"That won't be necessary."

The silence that followed broke her heart. More than anything she wanted to go to him, to hold him in her arms. She wanted to tell him what was in her heart… all of it…that she still cared for him…

"I tried to stray from Price and I was mistaken. I'm not ready to leave him. I'm not ready to start anything new. It has nothing to do with you and has nothing to do with your capacity to make me happy. I have no doubt you'd do everything within your power, but for now..."

"Serena, please don't say that," his beautiful velvet voice choke at her name.

"I have to tell you the truth, Sebastian. I should have told you the truth right from the start, but..."

"It's not too late."

"Sebastian, there's so much more you still don't know." While he'd had a glimpse of the woman she'd become under Price's thumb, he didn't really know the extent of her relationship with her master. Considering her brief liaison with Sebastian, she doubted he'd be able to take in all that encompassed that aspect of her relationship with Price. She was his, and there was no escaping that bond. If he was a vampire, she would be his sire. Like a protégé. It was emotional, psychological, physical, and encompass everything she knew. She couldn't escape it. Price was a part of her. Now she knew.

"I don't care," he persisted. "I want to know more. I want to know all that you are, all that you've been through. Don't underestimate my capacity to understand and accept it all." He paused, "I want to help you, whatever emotional hold he has on you, I want to break it. I want you to be able to stand on your own two feet and make your own decisions in life without being indebted to or under the influence of someone else. That's why I wanted you so much. I saw the potential in you, Serena. I saw the fire in you, the drive and desire. You can be set free. And all I want to do...all I can think about doing, Serena, is helping you reach that potential."

Serena felt her heart sink. She could hear Sebastian's shoulders slumping, hear how much he wanted to reach out to touch her to hold her through the phone...to give her strength. But she had to do this. She had to go back to Price, to keep Sebastian and everyone close to him safe.

"Like I said, it has nothing to do with you, Sebastian. My relationship with Price is what I need now. I'm sorry I didn't realize it sooner. I'm sorry I allowed you to become involved with me at all. I'd have never thought we'd..."

"I don't believe you."

Serena swallowed the ball of guilt and pain that crammed her throat.

"I am what I am, and I need a man like Price, who understands me. I'm sorry, Sebastian, but I've toyed with you enough, and now I just want to set the record straight. There's nothing between us. We've both had our fun, and now it's time to move on."

Sebastian's beautiful voice was hoarse. "Is that what you really want, Serena? Did our time together mean nothing to you?"

"Nothing, Sebastian. I'm not the innocent protégé you think I am…"

"But…" Sebastian said very softly. "It doesn't matter. I love you."

Her heart jumped into her throat, and she couldn't say anything back to him. She hung up just as tears streamed down her cheeks. It was for his own good, she argued. Price would go too far to keep Sebastian out of her life, and she had to save him now while she could.

She'd played subordinate to her master long enough and he'd taught her everything that made up who she was.

Now it was time for her to become the master.

Epilogue

Serena walked out of Price's penthouse, rode down the elevators to the lobby and walked pass the massive glass and chrome double doors leading outside to the little café around the corner. Serena was dressed in leggings, sandals, and one of Price's cashmere v-neck sweaters that smelled like musk and vanilla, like Price himself. She loved wearing his shirts, although they were much too large on her. With one of Price's leather belts, she ran it around her waist a couple of times before cinching it. She looked presentable enough, and since this was Southern California, no one would care if she was dressed differently.

She walked into the café and spotted the guy dressed down in a grey UC Irvine sweatshirt, dark jeans, and a baseball cap pulled down low over his eyes. Before heading over to him, she looked around, making sure no one was looking. As she got closer to the man, she couldn't help but smile.

Those piercing blue eyes peered lovingly out at her from under the cap. Even hidden under a cap, they shone like sapphires. Serena felt herself getting warm as she sat down next to the guy with the cap.

She didn't look at him when she said, "You look nice."

"So do you," the guy said taking her all in from head to toe. He leaned in closer to Serena until their shoulders were touching and took her hand, entwining his fingers into hers. "I miss you."

Serena sighed. She wanted to melt into him, rest her head on his broad shoulders while he held her. It had been a few days since she last saw him.

"Thank you for agreeing to see me," he said.

Serena took a shaky breath before saying. "I wanted to warn you and your family. I had to…"

"I thought you didn't care what happens to me," he said softly into her ears, tickling them so slightly like a gentle caress.

"That was because I wanted to protect you, especially in front of him."

The guy chuckled. "Good old…The Name That Should Not Be Spoken."

"He's still my master, and I've agreed to be with him," Serena said.

"It doesn't have to be that way, Serena. You're your own person, not whatever he wants you to be."

"But he's definitely more than obsessed with me. I don't know for sure, but I suspect he had something to do with you getting sick at the dinner, amongst other things."

"Then I have him to thank for bringing us closer together." He pulled Serena close enough that she was nearly sitting on his thighs. He bent down and kissed her neck."

"Sebastian…" Serena wanted to jump into his arms.

"Let's get out of here and go to my place, Serena. I miss you. You have no idea."

He stood up, bringing Serena to him. As soon as they rounded the corner, Sebastian pulled Serena into his arms, while kissing her with as much passion as he can.

When they finally broke apart, they were breathless and staring at each other.

"I take it that you forgave me for not telling you about my hang ups," Serena said.

"As long as you're in my arms now, that's all that matters," Sebastian led her to his Roadster, opened the passenger seat and helped her in before sliding into the driver's seat next to her.

"For now," Serena said. "I'm technically Price's, but..."

"You are not going back to that man," Sebastian growled angrily.

"But if he doesn't get what he wants, he'll make sure you and your family pays dearly. I'd better go back," Serena said.

"Not if I can help it, Serena, not if I can give you the sun and the moon. I'm prepared to do so."

Serena fought back tears, as she gazed into Sebastian's determined eyes filled with such love and passion for her.

He was about to kiss Serena again when his phone rang. "What is it?" he asked, frustrated yet aroused. That expression wasn't there long, replaced by shock.

His facial expression changed again, displaying calm collectiveness.

"What is it?" Serena asked, never seeing Sebastian like that at all.

"My father's deal, the merger of Granite Gyms...something happened. It was formally cancelled seconds ago."

"Don't know how that's possible," Serena said.

"Why would it be canceled?" Sebastian asked.

"He knows I'm with him now. He's got what he wants. Why would he cancel the merger...unless he thinks he doesn't really have me," she said.

"This meeting with me," Sebastian asked. "Did he know about it? Could he have known about it?"

"Just that I did call you from my cell phone to meet with you."

Sebastian checked her phone and took it with him. "I'll have your phone checked to see if it's been tapped. Anything else?"

"I don't know," Serena said. "Maybe my laptop or emails. Price can be very possessive. He did go through all my things once when I went on a weekend trip with some girlfriends while he was away on business, and found him fuming and outraged when I returned."

Sebastian took Serena's hand and pressed it to his lips. "I would never do that to you, Serena, no matter how much I want you as mine. I still do. I don't know if I can ever stop wanting it." He kissed her knuckles and held her hand tight against his chest.

Serena leaned over and kissed Sebastian on his lips before he pulled her closer to kiss her thoroughly. "I have to go back to him, Sebastian. I can't explain it, but I care for him, too. I know he's obsessed with me, but I have to see what else is he planning. Don't worry about me, Seb, I know Price so well. I know what makes him tick. I've learned so much from him, now's my turn to turn things around…" She kissed him again before stepping out of the car. "I'm going to assume my studies at school, Seb. And if you could, I'd like for you to become my formal official adviser on paper. We can't be lovers, we can't have a secret advisership or whatever it's called. Everyone, especially Price, should know you and I are strictly student and teacher."

Seb's mouth fell. "Are you sure about this?"

"Yes," Serena said. "For Price to accept that I'm truly his, we must do this. It's a small sacrifice to pay for the long term. I love Price, and I will do whatever I can to help him get over this hold on me, but I need my freedom, too. School's given me a second chance, and I'm not going to quit because someone's supporting me."

"Good," Sebastian said sadly. "I'll at least get the satisfaction of being able to see you and help you along in your studies." He sighed, before pulling her to him, his hands in her hair as he held her tight, his lips roving along her cheeks and throat before moving to her lips. "I'll get to see you again, and that's what matters now." He pulled back and got into his car. "I'll be seeing you on campus, Miss Singleton."

"Take care, Professor Sorensen," Serena said, a single tear flowing down her cheeks. *Good-bye Sebastian.*

The Innocent (Volume 2, The Protege)
July 2013

Excerpt from BOOK 1 of the

MASTER CHEFS SERIES ™

Devour Me

For Age 18 and up

kailin gow

Prologue

Jessica Cummings bit her lower lip as an excited thrill shot through her. Her taxi pulled up in front of the apartment building she'd be calling home for the next little while… if all went well.

Just around the corner was the International Institute of Culinary Arts, and her future, her dream of joining the ranks of top chefs.

"Jess? Are you still there?"

"Oh, Mom," Jessica shouted gleefully into her phone as she pulled a few Euros from her wallet. "Yes! Yes! Oui! Oui! I'm just now arriving at my apartment. I'm so excited, Mom. Paris, can you believe it? This is more than I ever dreamed of."

"I know," Samantha said. "And I'm happy for you, honey."

Jessica heard the strain in her mother's voice. While she knew her mother was indeed happy for her, she also knew she desperately needed a helping hand back home.

"Mom, I won't let you down. When I'm through here, I'm going to come home a great chef and you'll see what I'll do with our little East Side restaurant. I'll turn it into the greatest place in all of New York City. Errol King is the best chef in the world and I hear he's a pretty good teacher, too. I'm going to soak up all the knowledge he has to offer. "

Samantha chuckled. "Yes, I've heard he is quite the teacher."

"Mom, just because the guy is young and good looking doesn't mean he can't be a good teacher."

"No, but it does mean a lot of young and impressionable young female students are going to have a hard time concentrating on cooking… a meal, that is."

Jessica grinned. Chef King was certainly charming. He'd even taken to showing off his charms in a recent print add wearing only his very brief briefs. Fanning her face, Jessica tried to put the heated image aside. "I've seen cute guys before, Mom. I'm here to work and nothing else."

Samantha let out a warm laugh. "That's funny. I could have sworn I saw a few magazines that talked about the young chef; a lot of interesting photos, too."

The sexually charged photos came back to Jessica's mind. "There were some very interesting articles with those photos, Mom."

"Hmm, yes, I'm sure there was. Look, don't worry about the restaurant for now, sweetie. I'll do just fine. You have fun in Paris and call me once you're settled in."

"Oui, oui!" Jessica paid the fare, grabbed her coffee and stepped out of the taxi. "I'll call you tonight."

She slipped her phone into her purse as the taxi driver pulled her bags out of the trunk and set them on the curb. He nodded and mumbled as he made his way back into his cab.

"Thank you," Jessica called out. "Merci!"

As she turned to negotiate getting her bags up into her new apartment, a rambunctious chocolate Lab came around the corner and slammed into her. With her warm and sweet coffee splattered across the front of her dress, she looked at the dog with affectionate reproach. "And where are you going at such a speed?"

The big dog sat and looked woefully at her, his big, dark eyes begging her forgiveness.

"*Ah, mon Dieu. Javier, mais que fait tu la?*" An older man came up to Jessica, an empty dog collar hanging from the end of a short leash. "*Milles pardons, Mademoiselle.*"

"I'm sure he didn't mean any harm, sir." Though she understood little French, it was easy to see he was dismayed by his dog's behavior.

"*Mais, il à tout renverser votre café.*" He quickly slipped the collar around the dog's neck then took Jessica by the elbow. "*S'il vous plait. Laissez-moi-vous acheter un bon café chaud.*"

Jessica politely disengaged herself, but the man persisted. He took her by the arm, chattering all the way as he led her to a nearby café.

"*Le moindres que je peut faire c'est de remplacer votre café.*"

Frustrated by her inability to understand him and confused by his actions, she struggled to free herself. "I'm sorry, sir, but I don't really understand French very well, but I'm fine. And my bags… my luggage is there on the…"

The gray haired man relented and released her arm, but put his hand to the small of her back and gently pushed her toward the coffee shop. "*Vous aller voir. Ici c'est le meilleur café du quartier*." The man pointed to the waiter.

"Really, sir, I have to get my things into my apartment and I have to register at the Institute. Please… What do you want from me?"

"He just wants to buy you a cup of coffee." The deep, velvety voice held a hint of humor.

Jessica turned to face the source and instantly blushed as she faced the young man who smiled at her so many times in all those magazines. In person, he was even more impressive; tall, strong and imposing.

He glanced down at her soiled dress. "I imagine he feels bad for his dog's faux pas."

"Oh." Jessica could think of nothing else to say. As the blush that heated her face intensified, she hoped he'd simply think she was embarrassed by the situation and not flushed by his horribly, terribly, debilitatingly excruciating proximity. He stood so close to her, she could smell him.

Damn, she thought. He even smells good; like a man who worked hard, but took meticulous care of himself. His sultry smile exposed perfectly aligned teeth that gleamed. His dark hair fell in thick curls to his shoulders and it wasn't hard to understand how he'd landed the brief brief's ad campaign. Dark, sexy and talented… perhaps even a spark of danger in his eyes; tempting danger.

Without realizing it, she'd leaned in closer to him and when her knees buckled slightly, he quickly took a hold of her arm and held her steady.

"You okay?"

"Yes, I'm fine." She got control of her emotions and straightened up. "I'm sorry. I should have studied a little more French, but…"

Errol looked at the older man. "Ca va aller, Monsieur. Merci."

"Il n'y a pas de quoi." The gentleman nodded at Jessica and turned to speak to a waiter, while holding his dog close to his hip.

"American, I take it." Errol looked pointedly at Jessica.

"Maybe." Taken aback by his question, she looked at him with a slightly defensive scowl. "What of it?"

"Nothing," he said with a chuckle. "I heard you mention you'd be a student at the Institute. It's been a while since an American has studied there. Most students are from Europe, some from Asia a few from Africa and the Middle East. We barely get a handful of Americans, and they're mostly men."

"Oh." For a moment she wondered if her American status was an asset or a bad disappointment.

"Having an American woman at the Institute is a delightful surprise." Heat smoldered in his gaze as he took her in. "I'm Errol, Errol King." He shook her hand. "I'll be teaching a class this semester."

"Really?" Jessica said, sounding more surprised than she ought to.

The older man returned with a steaming cup of coffee. "Voila."

"Oh, no. You don't have to…"

"You should take that" Errol whispered.

Jessica glanced at the man then back at Errol who nodded.

"This is Dr. Philippe Emanuelle, Head Administrator at the Institute." He turned to the man. "Dr. Philippe, this is a new American student at the Institute, a Mademoiselle…"

"Jessica, Jessica Cummings." She extended her hand to greet the prominent Frenchman. "I'm so pleased to meet you, Doctor." In the far reaches of her mind, a few French words came to her. *"Heureuse de vous connaitre, Docteur."*

"I think he wants to make sure you have your dose of caffeine before you get to the Institute."

"Oh." She accepted the cup of coffee. "Thank you. *Merci.*"

"After all, the Institute is the toughest culinary school in the world. We churn out the best... we're that good, but we do want to make sure everyone is well prepared to succeed... so, if caffeine is what you need, well, caffeine is what you'll get."

"I appreciate it, but it's not that dire a need." She held the cup up to show the man her appreciation and gently patted the dog on the head.

"Dr. Emmanuelle is very fond of taking Javier for a walk on his break. Every Friday he brings him to school then takes him to the park at the end of the day."

"I can understand why. On the taxi ride over I saw a beautiful park, and it's such a lovely day."

"A tout a l'heure." Dr. Emmanuelle nodded and led his dog out of the café.

Errol stepped closer to Jessica, his blue-eyed gaze intense and heated. "I suggest you take advantage of this lovely day while you can. Classes can be very challenging and demanding."

"You make it sound so hard. I love to cook and I'm sure I won't have any trouble keeping up."

"A passion for culinary arts is admirable and much needed, but you need more; determination, perseverance… stamina. This isn't fun and games. It's serious."

"I fully expect it to be… and I'm very serious about it. I want to come out of this a top chef.

"Good." He licked his lips while his gaze dipped down to the coffee stain of the front of her dress and down to her exposed legs.

The heat was suddenly more than she could handle and she stepped out into the fresh air. The moment she turned around to face him again, the heated intensity of his gaze sent a wave of arousal over every inch of her body. Her clothes seemed inadequate and she felt nude and exposed before him.

She knew the fabric of her bra was thin, as was the cotton of her dress. In addition to that, the thin cotton of her dress was plastered to the thin fabric of her bra with brown coffee. She didn't even dare to look down at the picture she presented him.

Could he see through all that thin fabric and see how aroused she was? Could he see the glow of perspiration on her skin, the sensual flush of her cheeks or the pulpy flesh of her lips?

"You know, you have the kind of passion I like seeing in my students." His gaze trailed over her body again. "I'm sure you'll do fine." He lightly touched his fingertips to her shoulder and leaned in closer.

For a moment she thought he'd kiss her and she didn't know is she should be shocked or elated.

"The first year's tougher than you think. The best way to ace your classes is to pay attention to everything the instructor does, and make sure you know what he or she wants."

A few short, sharp breaths escaped her lips before she could speak. "You don't say." She took a step back. "I had kind of planned on that."

Unable to endure his intoxicating presence any longer, she turned to walk away, but he pulled her back. "You have all these bags to bring up to your apartment?"

"Yeah, and I'm not really sure which entrance I'm supposed to take."

"I wish I could help you, but…"

She nodded her understanding. "It wouldn't be appropriate…"

"No," he said as he flashed a magnificent smile worthy of a Hollywood close-up. "I guess it wouldn't."

"Right." Jessica snapped out of the daze that had taken over her brain. He was to be her teacher for the next semester and here she was already drooling all over him. She put her hand to the handle of her large suitcase and dreaded lugging it around all alone.

"I'll see you in class." He turned to walk away.

"Mr. King," she blurted out before she could stop herself. "As inappropriate as it may be, I really do need your help. I could walk through this maze of apartments for hours and I have all these bags to…"

"Say no more." With a warm smile that seemed to say so much, he slipped his hand over hers and took her suitcase.

Devour Me (Book 1 of the Master Chefs Series)

For Age 18 and up

Coming Soon!

Want to Know More about *The Protégé Series*, Author Insight, Author Appearance, Contests and Giveaways?

http://authorkailingow.blogspot.com

http://www.kailingow.com

Talk to Kailin Gow at:

and

on Twitter at: @kailingow

Who Should Play What? Cast the Dream Cast of The Protege!

Visit Kailin Gow's Over 18 Blog to cast at:

http://authorkailingow.blogspot.com

Who should play who in The Protégé:

Serena Singleton

Sebastian Sorensen

Laura

Price Turnsby

Willow Brooks

Michael Brooks

Mrs. Brooks
283

The Protégé by Kailin Gow

Kaiser Sorensen

Marika Sorensen